She'd been too proud, too furious with him yesterday...

Had it only been yesterday that everything was different?

"You forgot this." He held out the flute to her as if that was really what happened.

"And you brought it to me. You're just thoughtful like that, aren't you?"

He smiled. "It's been said that thoughtfulness is one of my virtues."

"Alex, if you continue to be this *thoughtful*, I simply don't know what I'm going to do with you."

His gaze shifted to her mouth.

"I might be able to make a few suggestions."

Dear Reader,

Shakespeare may have said, "All the world's a stage...."
To me, however, all the world (and the people in it)
is fodder for a book. It's interesting how stories are
conceived. I've found inspiration in the most unlikely
places: the vision of a hand holding a drink over a
balcony railing, a Parisian street market, my brother's
work as an advocate for the homeless and the headlines
of the newspaper, to name a few.

Julianne and Alex's story came about when three ideas
collided. My daughter's flute teacher turned to me one
day and said, "Hey, why don't you write a story about
a flutist?" And I said, "Sure! Why not?" Around that
time, I'd stumbled upon a sad news story about a young
woman who was killed in the line of duty as she did
humanitarian work in Afghanistan, and an uplifting story
about an organization that was bringing music education
into the lives of inner-city children who couldn't afford
instruments and lessons. The three ideas melded and
emerged as *Accidental Father,* a story about three
unlikely people who become a family. Together they heal
and become whole through the redemptive powers of
love.

I hope you enjoy reading this story as much as
I enjoyed writing it. Please visit my Web site at
NancyRobardsThompson.com. I'd love to hear from you!

Warmly,

Nancy Robards Thompson

ACCIDENTAL FATHER

NANCY ROBARDS THOMPSON

Silhouette

SPECIAL EDITION

Published by Silhouette Books

America's Publisher of Contemporary Romance

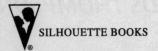

SILHOUETTE BOOKS

PLEASE RECYCLE
THIS PRODUCT IS RECYCLABLE

ISBN-13: 978-0-373-65537-3

Recycling programs
for this product may
not exist in your area.

ACCIDENTAL FATHER

Books by Nancy Robards Thompson

Silhouette Special Edition

Accidental Princess #1931
Accidental Cinderella #2002
*The Family They Chose #2026
Accidental Father #2055

Harlequin NEXT

Out with the Old, In with the New
What Happens in Paris (Stays in Paris?)
Sisters
True Confessions of the Stratford Park PTA
Like Mother, Like Daughter (But in a Good Way)
  "Becoming My Mother..."
Beauty Shop Tales
An Angel in Provence

*The Baby Chase

NANCY ROBARDS THOMPSON

Award-winning author Nancy Robards Thompson is a sister, wife and mother who has lived the majority of her life south of the Mason-Dixon line. As the oldest sibling, she reveled in her ability to make her brother laugh at inappropriate moments, and she soon learned she could get away with it by proclaiming "What? I wasn't doing anything." It's no wonder that upon graduating from college with a degree in journalism, she discovered that reporting "just the facts" bored her silly. Since she hung up her press pass to write novels full-time, critics have deemed her books "funny, smart and observant." She loves chocolate, champagne, cats and art (though not necessarily in that order). When she's not writing, she enjoys spending time with her family, reading, hiking and doing yoga.

This book is dedicated to Kathy Garbera
and Mary Louise Wells.
In celebration of sticking together through thick and thin.
Your friendship is a treasure.

Special thanks...

To Colleen and Nikolay Blagov for your guidance on the
inner workings of professional orchestras.

To Teresa Brown, Catherine Kean and Caroline Phipps,
talented writers and critique partners extraordinaire.
Extra special thanks (and many, many cups of coffee...
and a tiara) to Caroline, queen of the midnight edit.

And, as always, to Gail Chasan for being awesome.

And to Michael and Jen for loving me...
especially when I'm on deadline.

Chapter One

Paris, France

On Paris's eastern edge, north of Notre Dame Cathedral, concrete buildings reared up out of the Left Bank like stoic giants bucking to elbow out all that was good, familiar and charming about the City of Love.

Julianne Waterford glared at the incongruence from the taxi window, and tried to decide whether the jarring clash of new against old made Paris more approachable or if the contemporary intrusion simply ruined the magic.

She released a full-body sigh. Seeing this side of Paris on her first visit made her feel like Dorothy glimpsing the man behind the curtain.

This wasn't the Paris most first-timers toured. Because tourists didn't simply stumble upon this modern beast of a neighborhood. One had to have a reason to venture out to this part of the city.

Julianne's reason: an appointment. A significant, dreadful appointment. One glance at her watch made the wings of her heart drum a frantic staccato. She had about five minutes to arrive or she'd be late for that meeting—unless she changed her mind altogether and didn't show.

No. Being a no-show wasn't an option. She had to go through with it no matter how uncomfortable she felt about a face-to-face meeting with the louse who'd left her pregnant sister high and dry.

And, of course, Julianne would be on time.

As principal flutist for the Continental Symphony Orchestra, it had been ingrained in her that to be early was to be on time; to be on time was to be late; and to be late was to be fired.

Julianne Waterford was never late.

Because she'd been guarded about the reason for her meeting with Alex Lejardin, she at least owed him the courtesy of being prompt. Not that he deserved courtesy after what he'd done, but punctuality was, after all, Julianne's personal code.

She flipped through her French dictionary in search of words to ask the driver how much longer before they'd arrive. Despite the conversational French CDs she'd listened to when she learned the orchestra would travel to France, she'd never been comfortable actually speaking the language.

With that thought, she leaned forward to the driver. *"Pardonnez-moi, monsieur."*

The man glanced in the rearview mirror. *"Oui?"*

"Parlez-vous English, *s'il vous plaît?"*
Please speak English. Please.

"Oui—er— Yes, *madame.* I do."

Julianne sighed. *"Merci.* How much farther?"

"A few miles more." He scrunched up his lips in an oh-so-French way and shrugged. "Perhaps two minutes?"

"Merci, monsieur."

Thank goodness traffic was light; otherwise, she might be late, and to be late was to…well, it didn't bear thinking about. Sometimes, bad things happened even to people who were on time.

As Julianne eased back into the seat, she opened the manila file folder on her lap and glanced at the address on the press release she'd printed when she organized her journey. Only then did she realize her hands were shaking. To take her mind off her nerves, she read the words on the paper:

iWITNESS Appoints New Executive Director
Paris, France (June 25, 2008)—The Board of Directors of iWITNESS, the international watchdog of global human rights, takes great pride in announcing the appointment of Alexandre Lejardin as Executive Director.

Lejardin has a decade of experience in human rights law. Most recently, he served in Afghanistan as counsel for the World Human Rights Coalition (WHRC).

All it did was remind her that he'd left Marissa on the front line.

Lejardin: safe in a cushy desk job.

Marissa: dead in the line of duty.

Julianne folded the paper into a small square and closed her fist around it, training her attention on the ascending building numbers, which indicated that they might be farther away than a couple of blocks. She tapped a nervous cadence on the folded paper with her index finger.

Marissa trusted you, Alex. She loved you. How could you leave her like that?

Tears fogged her glasses and blurred the parade

of contemporary architecture that whirred past the taxi window. If Julianne couldn't get through the first sentence without crying, how in the world was she going to say what she needed to say without breaking down?

She should be better at holding in her emotions. Sometimes she could. Sometimes she couldn't. It had been a challenge since the day three months ago when she learned her sister was dead.

Three months ago today, as a matter of fact. Killed by a suicide bomber while working in Afghanistan advocating for war victims...

How fitting that the orchestra would bring her to the same city as Alex Lejardin on this anniversary of Marissa's death. It was as if fate were shoving her to stand up to Alex.

In memory of Marissa.

For Liam.

She closed her eyes against the tears. Everyone said the first year was the hardest. So far, the first quarter had been a struggle, three months that were one dirty smudge of events, one bleeding into the next. She'd had to get State Department approval to travel to Afghanistan. Once there, she'd identified Marissa's body and met Marissa's son in the same day. Becoming Liam's guardian had made it imperative that she somehow find the strength to go on—to work and care for the sweet little boy her sister had left behind.

Today's appointment—today's confrontation—would be one more event to fade into the miserable smudge. She had to do it.

In memory of Marissa. For Liam.

The cab stopped in front of a tall building that looked just as generic as the others around it.

Bingo. With two minutes to spare.

She shoved thirty euros at the driver, steeled herself against the riptide of emotion pulling at her insides, and got out of the cab, dodging people as she raced up the steps to the building's glass double doors.

Inside, it could've been any office building in any city. Dingy white linoleum floor, a bank of elevators, and a black magnetic sign with small white letters listing the businesses combined to bear no hint that the magic of Paris was only a car drive away. The iWITNESS office was on the sixteenth floor. As she joined the small group of people waiting for the elevators, she listened to the lyrical lilt of the French accents, catching a word here and there, but most of the chatter went over her head.

Too bad she hadn't been able to devote more time to learning the language or taken a class.

Once Liam entered her life, however, she had no time for much other than work and caring for the boy. First there was the race to find a suitable sitter—one she could trust, one Marissa would've liked, although Marissa, the supermom, had found a way to do it all. She had nurtured a baby and simultaneously aided victims of war. Julianne freely admitted she was not as altruistic, nor as good at multitasking as her sister. The plunge into instant motherhood hadn't come as naturally to Julianne as it had for Marissa. In fact, before Liam entered her life, Julianne had decided she didn't want to have children of her own. The only way she had been able to adapt to sharing her life with this little being was to cut all distractions except for her job as principal flutist for the symphony and her work with A World of Music, the charitable foundation that brought music into the lives of inner-city children. The focus of her existence, however, was caring for her thirteen-month-old nephew, who, much to her surprise, had stolen her heart.

Liam. Work.

Work. Liam.

Just like that, she'd eliminated the extraneous from her life. No more going out with friends or dating—not that she'd done much of either. No more nights watching favorite movies on television. She'd plucked the superfluous from her life like weeds from a garden. There was no time for movies when evening hours were spent sterilizing bottles and doing a baby's laundry.

Not that focusing only on Liam and work was so noble a sacrifice—the baby brought her a lot of joy. It was nice to share her life with him. And there was nothing quite like getting lost in a piece of music. For the most part, being a musician was a solitary job at heart.

Her work for A World of Music brought her into contact with a lot of people when she arranged for underprivileged kids to have free music lessons and the use of instruments. And of course, in the orchestra, she was part of the whole that made up the bigger picture—a cog in the gear that turned the machine. But the practice to get where she was today was a solitary endeavor. Julianne had gotten used to feeling alone in the crowd.

She and Marissa were so different.

Marissa had always had to give Julianne a push when it came to being introduced at parties. Extroversion had been her sister's great gift. Not communing with an inanimate instrument, but being accepted as part of the group anywhere and everywhere she went.

The memory made her eyes sting and her throat burn.

As the elevator dinged and its doors yawned open on the sixteenth floor, she blinked a few times and pushed her glasses firmly upon the bridge of her nose.

Looking around, she spied the sign that read iWITNESS, and tried to ignore the ugly feeling that urged her to turn around and go back to the hotel, to take the boy and go back to Washington, D.C., and remain *anonymous*.

But she wouldn't.

She couldn't.

No, just because Julianne hadn't fallen trippingly into motherhood didn't mean she loved her nephew any less. Because of that love, she would stay and do what should've been done a long time ago.

Alex Lejardin shoved aside the legal brief he'd been trying in vain to read all morning. Twice, he'd reached the bottom of the page and had no idea what he'd read.

His focus was nonexistent, which wasn't like him. He prided himself on his ability to shut out the world and zero in on his work. As the executive director of iWITNESS, he fought for people who had no other voice. People who deserved to have someone declare their trials, their injustices, their needs. The job demanded nothing less than *all* of him.

But today, he was distracted. Thanks to a faceless woman with a haunting last name.

He glanced at his watch. Julianne Waterford should arrive any minute.

He leaned back in his desk chair and laced his fingers behind his neck. He'd known one other person with the surname of Waterford.

Marissa.

The memory sent a thousand-watt jolt of grief coursing through him. His muscles tensed as a face came into focus from the far reaches of his memory. His friend. Marissa Waterford had been his friend. Never had he known a more selfless, magnanimous lady.

A living saint.

Once, they'd been as close as two friends could be—but still not as close as Marissa had wanted.

The memory made his gut clench, and he drew in a measured breath, grinding his jaw against the sadness.

Marissa had a sister back in the States…was her name Julianne? Alex racked his brain, trying to remember, but he came up empty.

All he could see was Marissa's face. The way

she'd looked the last time he saw her alive—devastated by the announcement that he was leaving Afghanistan, crushed by his rejection of her desire to turn their friendship into a different sort of relationship.

He rubbed his hands over his face as if to erase the memory. To no avail.

Julianne hadn't given his assistant any details when she'd scheduled the appointment. But cryptic messages weren't unusual at iWITNESS.

When people decided to expose human rights violators to organizations like iWITNESS, they were sometimes a bit cagey up front. In fact, often they remained nameless and faceless, mailing in unmarked tapes, pictures or discs.

Marie, Alex's assistant, and staff security guards operated under strict instructions not to push and risk scaring away informants. If someone seemed shady or up to no good, security was prepared to handle them, but in the time Alex had been with iWITNESS, there hadn't been a single incident. Lots of threats, but no action.

Alex had no reason to think Julianne Waterford's business was anything other than…business.

The intercom buzzed, and Alex jumped.

"Oui?" he asked.

"Alex, Julianne Waterford is here to see you," said Marie.

"*Merci*, Marie. Please send her in."

When Julianne entered Alex Lejardin's office, he stood to greet her. As she gazed up at him, her let-him-have-it confidence slipped a few notches and she clutched the manila folder for reinforcement. She'd seen a photo of him when she'd done her research, desperate to discover his whereabouts, and curious to know what kind of man abandoned his pregnant girlfriend in a war-torn country.

With his golden-streaked hair and mile-wide shoulders, he was just as handsome as he'd appeared in the picture circulated with the press release, but the two-dimensional photo hadn't prepared Julianne for his raw charisma.

He was tall, probably a good six-four. In his jeans and black sweater with sleeves pushed up to his elbows, he was dressed much more informally than she'd expected from a Parisian lawyer. Though those shoulders did a magnificent job of filling out that casual black sweater.

As he smiled and offered his hand in greeting, his charm was nearly palpable in the small, cluttered office, which wasn't nearly as fancy as she'd imagined.

Still, it was a far cry from the hovel in Afghanistan that Marissa and Liam had called home.

"Good morning, Ms. Waterford." His English was almost perfect with only the slightest turn of a French accent. "May I take your coat?"

She gave his hand a perfunctory shake and withdrew hers, shoving her fists in the pockets of her tan trench coat.

"No, thank you. I won't be staying long."

"Well, then how may I help you?"

Though she tried not to judge people, she'd learned enough about Lejardin from Marissa's stories to sum him up. This guy had superficial written all over him. He was too good-looking, from the obviously fake highlights in his hair—what kind of a man indulged in hair color if he couldn't even pay child support?—to his clean, trimmed fingernails, to the soles of his fine leather loafers.

She could see how the average woman would find him very attractive. But how in the world had Marissa fallen for a man like this? Her sister had always seemed above superficialities. It was simply the nature of her work as a foreign aid worker. Marissa was a humanitarian. She'd been attracted to men with a social conscience, men who put themselves on the front line to help others like she did.

Not pretty boys who hid behind a law degree in a Parisian office.

With a shaky hand, she took off her glasses and fought the urge to curl her lip. It was easier to look him square in his green-rimmed hazel eyes when her vision was slightly blurry. It distracted her from the way he was staring so intently at her.

"I'm not the one who needs your help." She held his gaze as his smile morphed from congenial into concern. "I'm here on behalf of your son."

The smile stayed firmly in place even as incomprehension clouded those hazel eyes. "Pardon? I must have misunderstood. I thought you said *my son?*"

Julianne shook her head. "No, you heard me correctly. I'm here on behalf of your son. Liam. Marissa may have let you off the hook, but I'm here to tell you that it is time for you to step up and take responsibility for your child."

She waited for him to say something. Anything. Or at least to act contrite, to show some emotion other than denial. But all he did was stare at her as if she were a mad woman.

Then he cleared his throat. "I'm sorry. You must have the wrong man. I do not have a child."

She frowned. Now he was making her mad. She hadn't come here to listen to lies.

"What kind of a man denies his son's existence? Do you think if you pretend he isn't there he'll go away? That may have worked with my sister, but she's gone now and so you have to deal with me. I'm not going to accept your shoddy excuses."

Alex was used to dealing with difficult people who flung crazy accusations. It was the nature of his position at iWITNESS—hearing reports of human rights abuse, verifying them and then exposing the heinous acts to the world and using his considerable contacts to apply political pressure so that the countries where these injustices happened were forced to stop the inhumane action.

What threw him was being the subject of the accusation. Especially when the allegation simply wasn't true. He didn't have a son. If he did, he certainly wouldn't deny his child's existence. It took him less than ten seconds to regroup.

"Ms. Waterford, please sit down." He gestured toward the chair in front of his desk. "Obviously, there's been a misunderstanding. Perhaps we can talk and clear up the confusion?"

She looked agitated. Even after removing her glasses, her blue eyes were a tempestuous sea that threatened to batter him with a storm of fury.

When she remained standing, he repeated, "Sit

down. Please." His words were softer this time. "You're Marissa's sister, aren't you?"

She leveled him with a dark, layered glare.

"Of course I am. I'd have no reason to be here otherwise."

He nodded.

Finally, she sat, smoothing the fabric of black slacks that peeked out from beneath the folds of her tan coat. Perching on the edge of the seat as if she didn't plan to stay long, she brushed her long, dark hair off her shoulder.

That's when he noticed her fingers were shaking.

She was obviously distraught—overwrought, even. Why else would she think he had a son? Why would she take it so personally?

With all the experience he had helping people who'd been through tragedy and lived through hell on earth, he should've known the perfect thing to say to Julianne to comfort her. But for a moment, words failed him. Until all he could say was, "Will you start from the beginning?"

She seemed to size him up for an eternity. "You and Marissa obviously had your differences."

Differences? "No. Not really. We were good friends. I was deeply saddened by her death."

Julianne silenced him with a raised hand.

"Good friends? That's all she was to you? A good friend? Is that how you rationalized leaving her and Liam?"

Alex heard the rising pitch of her voice. The woman looked ready to launch out of her chair at him. And for what? What on earth did he have to do with someone else's child?

"Who is Liam? Look, you've been talking in riddles since you arrived. I can't help you unless you help me understand. Are you in some sort of trouble? If you are, I will help you in any way I'm able. Because your sister was a very dear friend."

Friends. That's all they'd been. Yet, that old familiar pang coursed through him as memories of *that night,* that moment of weakness, that horrendous breach of good sense when he'd failed Marissa and jeopardized their friendship by crossing the line.

The way Julianne was looking at him, it was almost as if she knew.

Mon Dieu, would Marissa have told her sister?

Alex bit back an oath and hid his rising panic from Julianne by turning toward his desk, under the guise of sitting down.

When he was facing her again, he asked, "Is this Liam you speak of Marissa's son?"

"Your son." She looked exasperated, as if she wanted to yell, *That's what I've been trying to tell you.*

One time. He and Marissa had slept together one time.

But *one time* was all it took.

Obviously.

"How old is the boy?"

It took every bit of strength Alex could muster to keep his voice steady. His mind raced to do the math: If Marissa carried the baby nine months… and it had been nearly two years since he'd last seen her—since *that night*…the child would have to be just over a year to even possibly be his.

"He'll be fourteen months old on the twenty-eighth of this month," Julianne said. "I have his birth certificate right here. Your name is on it."

Fourteen months.

She'd said the words as though they were any words: "Nice weather we're having" or "I like dogs."

Fourteen months.

The time frame fit. Oh, hell.

As Alex Lejardin studied Liam's birth certificate he looked as if he'd seen a ghost. He sat there and stared at the paper for a long time—his features blank, the color fading from his sun-bronzed cheeks.

If she didn't know differently, she might believe this was the first he'd heard of Liam. But she knew better. Marissa had told her he knew. Marissa had said Alex left when he found out she was pregnant. That he had chosen not to be part of Liam's life. Marissa had come to terms with it, but Julianne wasn't going to let Alex get away with denying all knowledge of the boy. *The liar.*

"Look, don't worry," she said, mustering the strength to say what she came to say. She had to say it, just spit out the words, because the longer she danced around the issue, the harder it would be. "I'm not here to ask you to take custody of him. But a little financial support would certainly help the boy. Marissa had no life insurance, no benefits—another hazard of the thankless job that cost her her life."

She choked on the last word and bit her bottom lip to keep the tears at bay. She hated this—everything about it. Losing her sister. Having an orphaned nephew. And now, being forced to face Alex Lejardin with her hand out. Begging for money went against every fiber in her being. She was used to scraping by on her modest income with the orchestra. She'd even learned to plan ahead so that she survived during the times when the orchestra couldn't make payroll. That was the price she paid for her music, to do what she loved.

The life of the starving artist was fine for a single woman, but not for a baby boy who'd never asked for this fate in life.

Alex raked his hands through his hair. His eyes searched the small, cluttered room as if looking for a way out.

She waited stoically, watching him. The way he went to such great lengths to put on this act sickened her. She disliked him even more, watching him try to squirm his way out. Even though she wanted to tell him to save his act for someone more gullible, she knew she'd stand a better chance of gaining his support if she stayed calm.

She'd do it for Marissa.

For Liam.

"I wouldn't be here if it weren't an emergency." Her voice was steady now, as emotionless as she could render it. "I am a musician with a symphony orchestra, and the arts are…well, the arts are struggling in America. I simply want to be certain that Liam has what he needs. The money I'm asking for isn't for me; it's for his—"

Alex slammed his hand down on the desk.

Julianne flinched and leaned back into her chair.

Just a little. It was instinctual when a man this vibrant showed such emotion.

"Why didn't she tell me? All this time I've had no idea I have a child. *A son.*"

She met his gaze and the anguish she saw threw her off kilter. Then he looked away and squeezed his eyes shut.

He opened them after a deep exhalation.

"I'm sorry." He shook his head. "This is a lot to process." He shook his head again. This time it was as if he was trying to clear the confusion. "Obviously, we have a lot to talk about."

It took a while for Julianne and Alex to put the pieces together, but by the time she left two hours later, Alex was convinced of one thing: Marissa Waterford had lied to both of them.

She'd *lied.* How could this woman whom everyone had perceived as such a saint do such a thing?

She'd lied to her sister, painting Alex as a deadbeat who'd disavowed responsibility and run with his tail tucked between his legs when he'd learned Marissa was pregnant.

At the same time, Marissa had simply chosen not to inform him that she was pregnant with his son—even after he'd called her to try to make amends for *that night*.

That fateful night two years ago, when Marissa learned that Alex was leaving Afghanistan to accept the position with iWITNESS in Paris. She'd set out on a mission to convince him to stay, complete with mellowing alcohol and lots of female flesh on display. For one crazy moment, Alex had given in to the temptation she offered, but after they'd made love, he'd known he'd made a colossal mistake.

The next morning as he prepared to leave for Paris, she confessed she hoped that once they'd made love he'd stay. He told her he couldn't. He knew he could help more people in his new position in Paris than he could working the front lines. While he cared deeply for her, all he could be was her friend. He stressed how important she was to him, that he didn't want to lose her *friendship*.

But it was too late. The damage had been done.

Obviously stung, Marissa had insisted it was best that they made a clean break. Her goodbye was civil, chilly and punctuated with the firm click of his hotel room door as she walked out on him. After he'd settled in Paris, Alex had called her several times to salvage their friendship, but she'd made it clear she wanted no contact.

She'd told him that hearing his voice hurt. She'd asked him to quit calling. Not wanting to hurt her any more than he already had, he respected her wishes.

For two years. Then the sad news of her death had reached him through their mutual colleagues, and he'd grieved for the friend he'd lost, for the friendship he'd never been able to repair. Now, three months later, her sister was standing in front of him, informing him that Marissa had borne his child. It was almost too much to comprehend.

But one thing was certain: Even though he was never in love with Marissa, he would never have turned his back on her and their child…if only she'd informed him she was pregnant.

Now, as he sat in his dark office, lit only by the amber hues of the setting sun streaming through the lone window to the left of his desk, Alex knew how it felt for the world to spin out of control.

Or he might know if he weren't so numb.

Even so, with Julianne's utterance of those fateful four words—*You have a son*—nothing in his world would ever be the same.

The office was so still that the thoughts in his mind seemed to scream as he replayed their conversation over in his head: How, at first, neither of them had believed the other. While he'd confirmed that he'd been intimate with her sister, he couldn't bring himself to tell Julianne the details of what had happened between him and Marissa.

As she dug in, pouring on the guilt, accusing him of sidestepping responsibility, it crossed Alex's mind that Julianne might be an opportunist. Given his family's situation—less than two years ago his brother, Luc Lejardin, had married Sophie Baldwin, the heir to the throne of St. Michel, and had become the prince consort of that wealthy principality. Maybe Julianne smelled an opportunity to cash in.

But then she'd suggested a paternity test—insisted on one, in fact—before he could even bring up the idea himself. Then she'd asked for so little, and for that paltry amount to be administered with a strict accounting of how it was spent on the child. Even though his head cautioned him to proceed carefully, little by little, the evidence had mounted until his reasons *why not* fell away, leaving him with a gnawing sensation in the pit of his stomach that Julianne Waterford's claims just might be real.

He had a son and tomorrow he would meet him for the very first time.

Chapter Two

Julianne Waterford bounced the fussy baby in her arms as she waited by the octagonal pond in Luxembourg Gardens. She pointed to the numerous model boats that sailed on the water.

"Look, Liam. Aren't they beautiful?"

He squirmed and rubbed his eyes, and she was sorry for dragging him out on such a cold, windy March afternoon.

Yesterday, she'd agreed to meet Alex Lejardin in Luxembourg Gardens so that he could meet his son for the first time. The park was close to her hotel and it had seemed like a good idea…at the time.

After the tumultuous couple of hours they'd

spent sorting out the facts, they'd come to terms with the bottom line: Marissa had lied to both of them. They'd finally agreed the best thing to do at this point was for Alex to meet Liam.

Alex had suggested Luxembourg Gardens because it was "a kid-friendly place," where they could rent a small boat and Liam could watch it sail on the Grand Bassin. It might have been *a kid-friendly place* on a warm, sunny day. Today, however, Paris was cold and gray with a biting wind that wasn't friendly to anyone.

Maybe Liam would be more comfortable in the stroller? At least it would shield him from the breeze. She tried to lay him down, but he cried and reached for her, uttering "Mama," which completely melted her heart. So she held him.

Where was Alex?

Squinting at her watch—in her haste to get to the park, she'd forgotten her glasses—she saw that he was nearly fifteen minutes late. Her lips puckered in annoyance.

She bounced Liam and glanced around the sparsely populated park as if she expected Alex's blurry image to materialize out of the mist of her irritation. But the only people she saw were the handful of kids and adults sailing boats in the fountain, a couple canoodling on a nearby park bench and two strange fellows dressed in suits, wearing sunglasses standing in the distance.

Who did they think they were? The Men in Black?

The strangest thing was that they stood far enough apart from each other so that she couldn't tell if they were at the park together or not.

Then again, it was hard to discern details in the distance without her glasses. A protective sense told her it might be best to hold Liam and keep an eye on the creepy guys.

Ugh…great. She had half a mind to take Liam back to the hotel and tell Alex he'd have to come to them. Especially because Agents Kay and Jay were making her feel a little uncomfortable.

But before she left, she'd give Alex a few more minutes. Nobody was going to snatch her baby away from her in broad daylight.

Where in the world was Lejardin?

Careful not to take her frustration out on the baby, she gently hitched him higher on her hip, shifting his weight. She didn't realize it until after the fact, but his heavy eyelids had fallen shut and the motion must've startled him awake because he flung his head back and whined.

Anita Collins, the woman who watched Liam while Julianne rehearsed and performed with the orchestra, had warned her that Liam hadn't taken his morning nap. Even though Julianne was paying the cranky price for Liam's lack of sleep, it wasn't Anita's fault. The woman was the best babysitter a person in Julianne's situation could ask for. The wife of Graham Collins, the orchestra's oboe player, Anita was a grandmotherly type whose own kids had not given her grandchildren. She cheerfully, almost possessively, kept Liam while Julianne worked.

Because Anita traveled with her husband when the orchestra played out-of-town engagements, it was as if Liam had his very own nanny—with one important difference: Anita refused to accept monetary compensation. She said that the two kept each other company while the musicians worked and that was payment enough.

Julianne's parents had passed away years ago, and Marissa had been overseas for nearly as long. So friends like Anita and the rest of the orchestra were Julianne's only family. Her musical family had propped her up through the tragedy of Marissa's death. They'd secured substitutes to fill in for her when she'd traveled to Afghanistan right after Marissa was killed. And they'd stood by her on bad days. Sometimes it seemed as if the bad days would never end.

Music had always been her solace, the one orderly constant she could grab on to when her world was crumbling under her feet. Now she'd come to appreciate her musical family as much, if not more. They gave her a foundation in between the notes, during those rough, silent times when she didn't know how on earth she'd survive.

Then there was Liam, who, in the three short months he'd been with her, had become the center of her world. When she brought him home, her colleagues had lent her a crib, high chair, and playpen; they'd given gifts of baby clothes and offered gentle advice.

If not for her musical family...

Well, she didn't even want to contemplate the *what-ifs*. Reality was harsh enough. She blinked away the thought just as Liam unleashed another protest.

"I know, pumpkin." She kissed his temple, inhaling the sweet baby scent of him and tugged his coat zipper as high as it would go. "This isn't much fun is it? Even if you are going to meet your... daddy."

Saying that powerful word out loud caused a vague uneasiness to shimmer to the surface of the murky emotions that had emerged since meeting Alex yesterday.

She hugged Liam a little closer and squinted at the chestnut trees in the distance. When she spied a tall man with light hair among the people in the park, her stomach did a fast, nervous turn, but it only took seconds for her to realize it wasn't him. *Him.*

Maybe he wasn't coming.

Maybe he'd changed his mind.

Julianne shivered against a sudden gust of wind.

Yesterday, she'd left Alex's office convinced he was telling the truth. That he didn't know about Liam, but he did want to be part of his son's life. While that revelation helped where Liam was concerned, it tore a dark, gaping hole in the already-bruised place in her heart that ached for her sister.

Marissa, the sister she'd so admired, had lied about Alex's noninvolvement.

There was so much she still needed to sort out. She just couldn't process everything right now. She didn't know if being around Alex would help or make things more confusing. But even worse was the thought that he'd stand them up.

She wasn't asking him to share custody, she simply needed Alex to contribute and, for the boy's sake as he grew older, to show that he cared.

Time was of the essence. Paris was the last stop on the orchestra's European tour. The day after they played their concert, which was scheduled for tomorrow night, she and Liam would board a plane and head home with the rest of the musicians.

Suddenly Liam stiffened and erupted into a full-blown wail.

"Shh," she whispered gently. "Don't cry, honey." She reached into the diaper bag, which hung on the back of the stroller, pulled out a blanket and did her best to drape it over the boy with her one free hand. He burrowed down into it, resting his little head on the spot on her chest that ached for Marissa. His eyes were so heavy, yet with each gust of wind, with every peal of laughter and boisterous outburst of the kids merrily sailing boats in the fountain, he'd jerk awake and whimper.

She wanted to say, *"I know exactly how you feel, sweet boy. I want to cry, too,"* but instead, she whispered. "Let's go. We'll call him and reschedule."

She was turning to leave when she thought she spied Alex's tall, lanky frame hurrying across the green.

Or maybe we won't.

Alex waved to Julianne, who stood next to the Grand Bassin with a stroller by her side and what looked like a bundle of blankets hugged close to her chest. It had to be the boy—his son. Though he couldn't see him through the mound of cloth.

The thought that his child was only a few paces away unleashed an anxious sensation in the pit of his stomach, the likes of which he'd never known—even when his job had taken him to some unsettling situations.

They looked like Madonna and Child standing there, he thought, as he closed the distance between them.

"Sorry to keep you waiting," he said. "I was detained by a telephone call. I realized I had neglected to get your cell number, so I couldn't call and let you know I was going to be late."

Beneath a curtain of dark bangs, Julianne studied him with ice-blue eyes. She wasn't smiling, and the Madonna sweetness he thought he'd glimpsed as he approached was replaced by a demeanor that felt more remote. She seemed quite different from her sister. Marissa had been a passionate, strawberry blond ball of fire.

Granted, he was late and he'd only known Julianne for a single day, but his impression of her was that she was a woman of quiet reserve.

One of the things that made him good at his job was his ability to sum up people correctly in a flash. It was a gut feeling—a sixth sense—and usually it wasn't wrong. That's why he'd pretty much accepted Julianne's claims at face value. His gut told him she was telling the truth. Still, he was too accustomed to the importance of accurate fact-checking. After she'd left he'd set his sources on the task to verify that she was indeed Marissa Waterford's sister and that Marissa had given birth when and where Julianne claimed.

It all checked out.

Even Liam's blood type, which was compatible with his own.

"Calling would've been nice," she said, a cool edge to her voice.

Now, his gut was telling him this woman was a dark, proud ice queen—with stunning blue eyes. Although why that last bit should even enter his brain at a time like this, he didn't know.

"We were just about to leave," her voice was frosty. "Liam is cold and tired. He missed his nap today."

At the sound of his name, the boy lifted his head off her chest and peered out from under the blanket. When his eyes met Liam's for the first time, Alex was taken aback by the commotion that reared up inside him.

This was *his son.*

Right here.

The boy regarded him with sleepy brown eyes that were unmistakably Marissa's. So were the strawberry blond curls that sprang out from under the hood of his jacket as if attempting a brash getaway.

But what floored him was the dimple in the boy's little chin and a particular set of his tiny jaw. Alex wasn't sure if it was the penetrating way Liam stared at him or whether it was the intent way the boy pursed his lips, but something in his face gave Alex the sensation that he was looking at a living baby picture of himself.

His heart rate quickened and for a moment, all he could do was gape at the boy.

Alex was…a *father*.

This was his son.

Part him. Part Marissa.

A woman who'd lied and robbed him of his son's first year of life.

A woman who'd died doing humanitarian work.

How could a decent man hold a grudge against a dead woman?

Suddenly, a lump of emotion seemed to block his windpipe. Alex cleared his throat hoping it would allow him to breathe again. Then he sucked in a great gulp of air.

"Hi, Liam," he heard himself utter, unsure of where the words came from. "I'm your…father."

Unsure of whether to reach for him.

Or not.

Unsure of *how* to go about it if he did.

He'd never held a baby. His brothers didn't have kids yet. Luc and Sophie had been married a little over a year and had just announced that they were expecting their first child. Henri was a well-confirmed bachelor allergic to the thought of marriage, much less bringing another life into the world.

Though, obviously one didn't have to be married to have a…son.

"Would you like to hold him?" Julianne held Liam out to him, as if reading his earlier thoughts. "Here, he's kind of heavy."

Alex took Liam from her, and was surprised by how solid and sturdy the boy's small frame felt in his big, clumsy hands.

The boy squirmed. Alex brought him to his chest, shifting awkwardly, wrapping one protective arm around him and supporting his diapered bottom with the other.

His touch must've been too rough because the boy let loose a piercing wail that startled a flock of pigeons, causing them to kick up dirt and gravel as they took flight, scattering in all directions. Liam cried and reached for Julianne.

This wasn't going well at all.

"He's tired and cold." Her voice sounded apologetic. Even after yesterday's dealings, it was the first time she'd allowed him to glimpse a softer emotion in her.

"Right. Sorry." He handed the baby back to her. "I guess meeting here wasn't such a brilliant idea. I should've taken the weather into account when I suggested it."

There was an awkward pause as Liam settled down, snuggling into Julianne, resting his little head on her shoulder. Seeing them like that, it dawned on him that she couldn't be a complete ice queen if the boy was so fond of her.

Maybe he needed to step back and reframe the situation.

"Would you like to go get some coffee?" Alex suggested. "Perhaps Liam could have hot chocolate to warm him up."

She shook her head. "He's too young for hot chocolate."

"Really? I thought all kids drank hot chocolate or at least chocolate milk. I didn't realize there was an age restriction."

She looked at him as if he'd suggested giving the boy whiskey.

"Technically, I guess there's not an age restriction. If it's going in a sippy cup, it would have to be only tepid chocolate, not hot. But really, I'm simply trying to teach him good habits."

What the heck was a sippy cup?

"Is chocolate a bad habit?" He smiled hoping she'd realize he was simply trying to lighten the mood, not indict her. "*You* must not like it if you think it's so bad?"

"I didn't say it was evil." Her voice was hoarse with frustration. "I happen to like chocolate very much. But I have a hard time getting him to drink regular milk. When he has chocolate milk, he doesn't want the plain variety."

He quirked a brow at her. "So you *have* given him chocolate milk before?"

She leveled him with a murderous glare, and he knew he'd gone too far.

He held up his hands in surrender. "Okay, okay, I'm sorry. I'm just kidding with you." He studied his shoes for a moment, searching for the words to explain. When he looked back up their gazes locked. "Also, I'm a little nervous. You see, I've never done *this* before."

He gestured to the boy, who had fallen sound asleep on Julianne's shoulder.

"I haven't either." When she lowered her gaze to look at the sleeping baby, the image of Leonardo da Vinci's *Madonna* returned. She was a classic beauty with her dark hair and piercing blue eyes. How had this escaped him yesterday?

In an instant, the magnitude of all that had unfolded yesterday flooded back to him, answering his question.

As she looked up at him, she bit down on her lower lip, and a silent understanding seemed to pass between them. Neither of them knew what they were doing. Though she seemed to be a hell of a lot better at it than he was.

"Look, it's cold out here, and I should get him inside. The best thing for him would be to take him back to the hotel. He missed his nap this morning, and he's overtired. Would you like to walk back with us?"

"Sure. Would you like to take a car rather than walk?"

"If he'll stay asleep when I put him in his stroller, it would probably be easier to walk. The hotel isn't far."

Liam stayed sound asleep after Julianne laid him down. As Alex watched her cover the boy with blankets, tucking him in all snug and warm, a powerful emotion washed over Alex. He knew in an instant that his life had just changed.

Irrevocably.

Chapter Three

"Is this your first trip to Paris?" Alex asked Julianne as they made their way along the Boulevard St. Michel toward Julianne's hotel.

She was relieved that Liam had stayed asleep when she'd placed him in his stroller. Even though it was cold, the baby was warm and comfortable. Julianne wanted to walk back to the hotel rather than ride the short distance so that she could get some much-needed exercise. She'd been cooped up indoors for rehearsals and hadn't had a chance to soak up much of Paris. To be honest, she realized as she walked, she wanted more time to talk to Alex—to get to know him—er—Liam's father—because they'd have so little time together before she and the boy returned home.

"Yes, it's my first time here," she said. "I've always wanted to visit, but until this trip, the opportunity never presented itself."

He shot her a sidelong glance and a charming smile that made her a little nervous. A fun kind of butterfly-nervous that she didn't understand. Maybe it was being in Paris, or more realistically, maybe it was because Alex Lejardin had proven himself to be a different man than the self-involved cad she'd thought he was before she met him yesterday.

She offered him a shy smile and looked away, training her gaze on the storefront windows as she pushed the stroller along the sidewalk. The windows felt like a safe place to keep her gaze. Even though she could see his rolling reflection as it jumped from window to window as they walked by, sometimes their images made eye contact in the glass. He would smile or make a face and she would laugh—who knew he could be so funny? Other times he'd be looking straight ahead. When he wasn't looking at her, it would spark a strange disappointment that was equally gripping and unfamiliar.

If she didn't know better, it almost felt as though Alex Lejardin was flirting with her. Harmlessly.

Nothing sleazy or suggestive. Just simple *ooo-la-la,* man-to-woman attention that threw her off kilter and reminded her that she was a woman who was tempted to flirt back.

And wasn't that just like a Frenchman?

But her flirting muscles were terribly out of shape because she'd had no reason to exercise them in ages. So she stuck to the reflective "window flirting" until, as they passed a cute little dress shop, Julianne could've sworn she saw the Men in Black—the guys from the park—reflected in the shop window. A startled jolt shot through her. She stopped and whipped her head around to look for them.

But they weren't there.

"What's wrong?" Alex asked.

"Nothing." As she stood there, she did a slow, sweeping scan of the wide street that was teeming with pedestrians and cars. It would've been easy for the Men in Black to get lost in the crowd. "Well, actually, strangely enough, I thought I saw someone…"

"Someone from the orchestra?"

She shook her head. "A couple of guys I thought I saw lurking around at the park when we were waiting for you. It just startled me for a moment." Hearing herself insinuate that someone might be following them sounded a little crazy. "It must have been a trick of the light on the glass."

Alex glanced around, as if he were trying to pick them out of the crowd, but then his eyes snared hers again, the natural light made the green rim around the iris even more pronounced. It was like looking at a kaleidoscope of amber and honey, moss and tortoiseshell.

"May I ask you a question?" he said.

She blinked and looked away because she realized she'd been staring into his eyes too long. "Sure."

She bent down to check on Liam, to adjust his blankets and make sure he was still sleeping soundly. He was, and he looked like, an angel. The sight of him warmed her from the inside out.

"Something you mentioned yesterday at the office keeps lingering in my thoughts. You mentioned that in America the arts are struggling for funding. I'm just curious, how is it that your orchestra is able to tour Europe if funds are so tight? I'm fascinated by this. Do you mind talking about it?"

Now he was the one staring intently at her, and she forced herself to look him in the eyes as they started walking again.

"A sponsor, of course."

He nodded as if he'd already guessed as much.

"Was it a European sponsor?"

So many questions. But that was fine. Kind of nice, actually. Since they'd left the park he'd been making a genuine effort to engage her. She appreciated it, especially because small talk had never been her forte. It was nice how easily they seemed to get along now that the initial ice was broken. Their getting along would be important in the future since Alex seemed interested in being a part of Liam's life.

"Yes, we were fortunate to be invited on a six-city, European tour arranged by the Pedersen Foundation. It's an arts organization based in London that raises money to send orchestras on tour. Their mission is to raise awareness of the arts and culture in other nations. The concert tomorrow night is the last performance on the tour, and then we return home the day after tomorrow. It's been the trip of a lifetime. Would you like to come to the concert? I can leave tickets for you at will call."

"I'd love to come, but I'm happy to purchase my tickets. To support the arts."

"That's very generous of you, but comps are one of the few benefits of my job. I haven't had anyone to share them with. It would be wonderful to be able to use them once on this tour."

It dawned on her that he might want to bring a

date, which put a different kind of butterfly feeling in her stomach.

"How many tickets should I leave for you?"

"Now it's my turn to say that's very generous of you. One ticket would be very much appreciated. Perhaps we could have a late dinner after you're finished? If it wouldn't interfere with Liam or another engagement you might have with the orchestra or with the Pedersen Foundation? It would be a great time to discuss plans for Liam."

Of course he only wants to be informed of my plans for the boy. I'm thrilled that he's interested and will definitely keep him apprised of everything that happens in Liam's life.

"That would be lovely. Thank you. As far as I know, there's nothing scheduled for after the concert. Although things sometimes come up last minute. Would you mind keeping the plans flexible?"

Alex nodded his consent. "Too bad my brother wasn't aware of your tour. You could've come to St. Michel."

"St. Michel? As in, the Boulevard St. Michel?"

She gestured around the street on which they walked.

"No." Alex laughed. "I'm talking about the

island. It's a separate principality right off the coast of France."

Despite the cold, Julianne felt heat fan across her cheeks. Even though she felt silly and decidedly uncultured, like an uneducated geography failure— his voice was a soothing rich mellow timbre with the tones of a well-played cello.

"Don't worry, many people have never heard of it" he said. "We don't hold a major car race like Monte Carlo does to attract tourists. I'm from St. Michel originally. My brother is the state's minister of arts and culture."

"St. Michel. Of course," she said, suddenly remembering. "Last year an American woman made headlines when she discovered she was the long-lost heir to the throne."

Alex nodded. "But I'll bet you didn't know that that woman, Sophie Baldwin Lejardin—the queen of St. Michel—is my sister-in-law."

Julianne stopped in her tracks. "Are you kidding?"

Alex shook his head. "Why would I kid about something like that? She married my brother, Luc."

"The minister of arts and culture?"

"No. Luc was formerly the minister of protocol.

Now he is the prince consort. My middle brother, Henri, is in charge of arts and culture."

Julianne stared at him with eyes so large and blue that for a fleeting moment he wanted to swim in them. Until he remembered himself, and the sobering fact that she was Liam's aunt, Marissa's sister. Not a woman to be trifled with. Perhaps rather than acting like an imbecile and making faces at her in the glass to hear her laugh, it would be best to direct his gaze straight ahead.

Not at her.

Not at her blue eyes.

Perhaps at his son sleeping in the carriage.

He also decided that it would be a good time to begin easing into the fact that she undoubtedly did see the security agents who were following her. Given the dangerous nature of his job of fighting human rights violators—who were another breed of terrorist—coupled with the fact that Liam was related to the royal family of St. Michel, Secret Service agents would now be a permanent presence in her and Liam's lives.

Arranging for Julianne and Liam to be guarded was among the first things he'd done once Julianne's story checked out.

The last thing he wanted was Liam or Julianne

to be used as a pawn in the sick game of world politics. Of course, that posed another problem: Liam would be much safer in St. Michel rather than in the States with his aunt.

Funny, twenty-four hours ago, the last thing he would've wanted was to be saddled with a child. Now, the thought of protecting his son was his greatest priority.

He simply needed to figure out how to let Juli-anne know the magnitude of the situation without scaring her.

"How long have you been with the orchestra?" Alex asked

"Three years." Inwardly she cringed at her short, closed answer. Really she needed to make a better effort at keeping up her end of the conversation.

"Where else did you perform on this tour?"

"Rome, Milan, Barcelona, Madrid, Nice and now Paris." She checked off the cities on her fin-gers as she named them. "Actually, it's my first time out of the U.S. Marissa was the adventurous traveler in the family."

They strolled silently for a few moments, Ma-rissa's memory walking between them like a silent ghost.

There were so many questions she wanted to

ask him about his relationship with her sister: How
did he and Marissa meet? What had they meant to
each other—or what had she meant to him? She'd
already heard Marissa's side of the story, but Alex
had been a bit closed about his relationship with her
sister, saying only that they were "good friends."

Good friends who had a baby?

The thought knocked the breath out of her. Before Marissa died, it had been three years since
Julianne had seen her sister. They were both busy.
Marissa had her work; Julianne had just landed
the position with the orchestra. They talked often,
e-mailed more frequently. They'd fully intended
to see each other—for the holidays or one of their
birthdays. Or when Liam was born…

The wind whipped her hair across her face,
making her eyes water. She stopped and pretended
that something had blown into her eye.

"Are you all right?" Alex asked.

"Yes, I'll be fine. Just give me a moment. Let
me close my eyes and see if it'll water itself out."

Actually, no, she wasn't fine. She was a cow-
ard. That was the long and short of it. She'd been
too afraid to venture to war-torn Afghanistan to
be with her pregnant sister when Marissa needed
her most, when she was giving birth. Julianne had

rationalized it—written it off with valid excuses. Perfectly valid, rational, reasonable excuses.

She had performances. Her orchestra mates needed her. She couldn't just up and leave. They were planning this European tour, rehearsing night and day...and even though she wouldn't be there when Liam was born they could meet in Paris when Julianne was here with the orchestra. Blah, blah, blah, blah, blah...as if they had all the time in the world.

Three years since she'd seen her sister. *Three years.* And now it was too late. Julianne realized, as she stood there with Marissa's baby in a stroller and the man who'd fathered the child standing beside her, that even though she thought she and her sister were close, she really hadn't known Marissa at all.

And now she never would.

"Here, let me have a look."

"No. I'm okay. " Julianne waved him off and turned away from him again. She sucked in a deep breath, summoning her composure.

A moment later, she felt stronger and swiped away the remaining tears that somehow had managed not to brim over.

She walked closer to a storefront window to check her reflection in the glass hoping her mascara was still in place. But it wasn't her own face that caught her eye—it was the old, battered flute haphazardly tossed in with the rest of the junk in the so-called antique shop window.

It was a Bundy. Identical to the one she'd started with in junior high school. It was an oldie, but certainly not an antique. And not very valuable. In fact, she'd seen similar models on eBay for as little as $5.00—though flutes at that price were few and far between and she grabbed them up as soon as she found them. It would certainly be worth checking this one out. There were always more kids who needed a chance to make music than there were instruments.

She glanced at Liam, who was still sound asleep, snuggled down into his blankets.

Yes, it would definitely be a find for one of the kids who received help from her A World of Music foundation. She turned to Alex. "I know this is crazy, but would you mind staying out here with Liam while I go inside? I want to check on this flute in the window."

He looked confused. "For you?"

She laughed, feeling more like herself again. "Oh, no, not for me, for one of my students. Liam seems comfortable and I'll only be a moment."

Alex nodded. "Sure, take your time."

* * *

Alex knew about Julianne's charitable foundation, A World of Music. The investigator had given him a brief outline of it in Julianne Waterford's dossier when Alex had ordered the background check. No wonder she was so good with kids, he thought as he watched her through the shop's glass door.

Anyone who was talented enough to play with a symphony orchestra that toured the world, anyone who cared enough to round up musical instruments and volunteer teachers had to be good with children. And have a heart the size of the globe.

Liam was lucky to have an aunt like Julianne.

At least she'd still have plenty of little ones in her life when Liam went to live in St. Michel. It seemed wrong for her not to have children in her life somehow.

As Alex watched Julianne haggle with the shopkeeper, he wondered why she didn't have kids of her own. The report had indicated she'd been married briefly to a man who had also been a musician in the Continental Symphony Orchestra. After their divorce he left the group. Since him, there was no evidence of other romantic interests in her life. Perhaps she'd simply chosen to focus on her career. God knows she seemed busy enough with the orchestra, the foundation and now, Liam.

Even though they seemed to click, Alex imagined that people took Julianne at face value. She didn't seem like the easiest person to get to know. Sometimes reserve was mistaken for aloofness. Yet she was quite charming when given the chance.

She wasn't shy, as evidenced by the way she'd burst into his office to defend her nephew, and she obviously had no qualms about getting up on stage and performing her music in front of large audiences.

Hmm... The woman was a study of contradictions.

Although he couldn't hear what she and the shopkeeper were saying, she seemed to be holding her own. The man must've spoken English, because Alex witnessed a lot of back-and-forth talking and some emphatic headshaking and gesturing on the part of the shopkeeper, an old man who looked as antique as some of the relics in his cluttered shop.

Someone honked a car horn and Liam startled awake crying. Loudly.

Oh, great.

Clumsily, Alex picked up the baby, and that only seemed to make him cry louder.

Much to his relief, an empty-handed Julianne exited the shop a few moments later.

"Oh no, poor baby," she said. "What's wrong?"

At the sound of her voice, Liam turned and held his little arms out to her.

"A car horn startled him," Alex said.

"Here…" Her voice was soothing as she took the baby. Liam stopped crying and smiled at her through his tears.

"Ma Ma," he said.

Ma Ma? He called her mama?

For a moment, Alex worried about how taking the boy away from Julianne would affect his son.

Mama…

He blinked away the thought. Liam was young, and he was also a sitting duck for a kidnapping. Sending him to St. Michel was the best thing for him, even if he couldn't expect Julianne to drop her life in Washington, D.C., and go with him.

She has her foundation and her job with the orchestra; a full life and important commitments.

"The old coot must be insane to think he can charge $500 for that flute." Her words chased away his thoughts. "If he's not crazy, he's unscrupulous. If he tricks someone into paying that kind of money he'll be guilty of robbery."

They resumed their trek toward the hotel.

"How much did you offer him?"

"I was willing to go as high as $30. But even that was high."

Alex shrugged. "Well, if he was asking $500 apparently he didn't agree."

"Maybe it's because I'm American, because my French isn't very good? Do you think?"

"Who knows? It's hard to say since I wasn't in there with you."

That wasn't the only thing that was hard for him to say. She was set to leave Paris the day after tomorrow. At dinner tomorrow night he had to tell her that she'd be leaving without her son. No— without his son!

Her nephew, who called her, "Ma Ma."

Chapter Four

"I'm speechless," Alex's brother, Luc Lejardin, uttered through the telephone receiver.

Breaking the news about Liam to the family was the first step in devising a security plan to protect the boy and to ensure Alex didn't lose his son for good. Because Luc had once been the head of St. Michel's national security before his marriage to Sophie, the newly crowned Queen of their country, Alex figured talking to Luc first was the best place to start.

Thank God Luc's loss of words was only momentary. Before Alex could begin explaining how he'd discovered he was a father, Luc was bombarding him with a barrage of who-what-why-where questions. Not the least of which was, "When do I get to meet my nephew?"

"That's a good question," Alex said. "Julianne, his aunt, is set to go back to the States tomorrow."

Luc blew out an urgent breath.

"Is that what you want?"

"I don't know. I mean, no, it's not what I want. I don't want to lose any more time with my son. But realistically, I can't do the work I'm doing and raise a child alone."

There was a long pause on the line, but Alex could almost anticipate his brother's next question.

"Have you considered the security issues associated with sending the boy back to the States? Especially given the Vonisian issue?"

"Of course," Alex said. "That was one of the first things I thought of."

Through his work with iWITNESS, Alex had recently exposed heinous acts of genocide committed by a group of rebel militants in the small, war-torn European country of Vonisia. Working with informants, Alex had gathered enough evidence against Vonisian rebels to involve the United Nations. Even though the case would soon be up for review by the International Criminal Tribunal, underground Vonisian militants were still carrying out monstrous acts of ethnic cleansing and issuing brazen threats against those trying to end their illegal, brutal rule and bringing them to justice.

Alex was at the top of their hit list because he'd been the driving force behind the victims' fight for human rights. Despite numerous threats, there'd never been an actual violent incident aimed at Alex thanks in large part to his own private security team. However, now that Liam was in his life, it made Alex all the more vulnerable. The people he exposed wouldn't hesitate to take his child hostage and use the baby as leverage against him. They'd done it to their own countrymen enough times for Alex to know that was their favorite mode of operation.

"You can't allow the aunt to take Liam out of France," Luc said. "It's just not safe. Plus, if you do, you might have a harder time getting him back if she decides to play hardball."

The image of ice queen Julianne that first day she'd arrived at his office, fighting for Liam's child support, snapped into focus in Alex's mind's eye. He'd experienced firsthand how strong her "mama bear" instinct was and how fast she'd rear up when it came to protecting the boy. Still, even though she could be fiercely protective, she'd be no match against conscienceless monsters intent on cleansing the world of people who weren't like themselves, including anyone who tried to stop them.

Yes, it would be in everyone's best interest for Liam to stay in Europe where he could have the highest degree of protection with the least amount of interference from St. Michelian Secret Service. But it was a double-edged sword: It would be hard on the boy to be taken away from Julianne, the person he considered *Mama*. Alex knew what it was like to have his mother ripped out of his life; he'd lost his own mother when he was a child. It was heartbreaking to think of hiring a stranger to care for Liam when the baby loved Julianne so much. On the other hand, leaving Liam with Julianne was exposing both of them to potentially life-threatening danger.

And the idea of Julianne being in harm's way roused his own protective instincts. He grappled with whether he should tell her about the specific dangers, but decided it would only alarm her. For now, all she needed to know was that the nature of Alex's job posed danger to all who were in his life and that danger increased for Liam since he was a member of the royal family.

"You do want to be a part of your son's life, don't you?" Luc asked.

"Yes, I do. There are just so many things I still need to sort it out. I travel so much, I can't exactly take him with me or stick a fourteen-month-old in a boarding school."

"Bring him to St. Michel," Luc offered. "The palace is one of the safest places on earth. He'd be well-cared for among family. Maybe we'll even get to see you more often since Henri and I aren't enough to get you back here regularly."

"Liam's cuter than you are." Mixed emotions washed over Alex. It was exactly the offer he'd hoped to receive from Luc—even if Alex hadn't realized it when he called. Despite how close Alex and his two brothers were, asking either of them to raise his son was a tall request.

So, for Luc to offer…

"But then there's the matter of Julianne." Alex squeezed his eyes shut and pinched the bridge of his nose. "I know for a fact neither she nor Liam will be happy being separated."

"She's welcome to come St. Michel, too. Believe me, there's plenty of room in the castle."

"Easier said than done," Alex said. "She has a career and a charitable organization she's involved with. I doubt she'd go for it."

"Even if it was a matter of the boy's safety?" The pitch of Luc's voice rose at the end of the sentence, as if such hesitance was unthinkable.

"I don't know, Luc. Like I said this is all new. I'm still getting my mind wrapped around it. All I know for sure is that she's fiercely protective of Liam."

Alex leaned back in his office chair and stretched his legs out under his desk.

"Has she legally adopted him?" Luc asked.

"According to my preliminary investigation, no. The court has simply appointed her his legal guardian."

"Good. That is very much in our favor. You are his father. Any idea if this Marissa named you as the father on his birth certificate?"

"Yes, she did."

Alex picked up Liam's file, the most important item on his desk. He thumbed through the documents, most of which—including Liam's birth certificate—he'd copied the day of Julianne's first visit. Other documents had been obtained during the background check his investigators had performed.

"You're in a very good position, then," Luc said. "Is it an official birth certificate?"

"No, just a photocopy."

"It won't be difficult to get our hands on a legal copy," Luc said. "Send over everything you have and I'll get the St. Michel legal team to formalize everything. Liam is family, Alex. We'll make sure you get to bring him home where he belongs."

Still, even though he'd gotten everything he'd wanted from that call, Alex felt terrible after he hung up the phone. Was taking his son away from the only mother he'd ever known really in Liam's best interest?

Then he remembered the video he'd obtained of the Vonisian militants torturing a captive.

No, taking Liam to St. Michel was for the best. For his son and for Julianne. Somehow, he'd have to make her see things his way.

The message from Alex said that he had a surprise for Julianne, and asked if she could meet him for lunch at the Café des Capucines, just down the street from the Opéra Garnier.

It was the day of the concert, and her schedule was full. The morning was packed with rehearsals and photographs and last-minute fine-tuning for the evening performance. Still, when she'd tried to beg off, he'd told her it was urgent, that he really would appreciate her making the time.

"You have to eat," he'd said. "Let's get lunch."

She had a nagging feeling the *urgency* centered around Liam. Surely, given how attentive and interested in the boy as Alex had been, she couldn't imagine the surprise would be anything bad...

After all, he said he had a *surprise* for her.

Weren't surprises usually good?

She certainly was pleasantly surprised when she arrived at the busy café and found him waiting for her at the most charming, most private table in the place. She only had about an hour before she had to get back to the theater, so it was a definite plus that he already had their table.

He looked nice in khaki pants and a dark blue button-down. His hair was gelled so that it stood up a little, just enough to be fashionable, but messy enough to look like he wasn't trying too hard. The sight of him made her smile as she wound her way through the crowded maze of tables toward him.

He looked up from the menu and spotted her, getting to his feet to greet her.

"You look beautiful," he said. "Thank you for meeting me."

He put his hand on her shoulder and leaned in and kissed her on the right cheek. Her face warmed and her heartbeat sped up. Even though she knew the kiss was strictly a polite custom, he hadn't greeted her like that before. Another nice surprise, she thought as he pulled out her chair and she settled herself.

It wasn't until she was reaching for her napkin that she noticed the battered Bundy flute case on the table next to her place setting.

"What is this?" she asked, even though she knew good and well it was the flute she'd looked at yesterday in the Boulevard St. Michel junk shop.

Alex sat across from her looking very pleased with himself.

"It's your surprise," he said. "Though I think you already know what it is. Open it. Give it a look and see if it's still as you hoped it would be."

She shot him one last quizzical look...an un-spoken *why...?* Before she placed the case on her lap and did just that.

"Alex, why did you do this?"

He shrugged. "You mentioned it would help your students."

A warm glow spread through her, and as a heart-breaker of a smile spread over his face her pulse jumped again. Unnerved, she struggled for a way to get back on solid ground. Especially because what she wanted to do was jump up and hug him. That's what Marissa would've done. But that wasn't Julianne's style. By the time she'd finished think-ing through the act in her head—seeing the flute, imagining jumping up while squealing a thrilled thank-you-so-much-Alex, throwing her arms around his neck, possibly even planting a kiss of gratitude on his full bottom lip—the spontaneity had passed.

The moment was gone.

"Please let me reimburse you," she murmured. "But please tell me you didn't pay the price that bandit was demanding."

"*Ahh.*" He waved away the suggestion. "Think of it as a charitable contribution to your foundation. Though I did manage to get the local discount." He winked at her. "In all seriousness, I simply went in with proof of what the flute was selling for online and offered him double that amount. It worked out to about the same cost after you factor in shipping and handling."

She was quite touched by his gesture, and for a moment, the words to relay her gratitude escaped her. She was relieved when the server, a petite blonde wearing a white button-down and black slacks with a white apron tied around her waist, approached and started speaking to them in French.

When Alex relayed that the special of the day was salade niçoise, Julianne was delighted to discover it was a dish she'd been dying to try.

She ordered it and iced tea. Alex ordered *boeuf bourguignon* and suggested they share a bottle of wine.

"I know it would be delicious with the salad, but I still have a long day ahead and if I drink, I might fall asleep at my music stand."

She closed the flute case and set it on the floor by her feet.

"You're still coming to the concert tonight, aren't you?"

He leaned forward, as if he was interested in her every word. "I wouldn't miss it."

The relief that flooded through her was unsettling. It struck her like whiplash, flipping her thoughts first one way, and then back in the other direction. She reached into her purse and pulled out a small, white envelope, happy to hand it to him rather than leave it at the impersonal will call window. "Here's your ticket."

"Thank you." He smiled at her and she lost herself for a moment. There was more to Alex Lejardin than she'd initially given him credit for. The proof was in how he treated his son. And in his purchase of the flute for her music foundation, which proved that he was not only generous, but warm-hearted and kind, too. He was also funny and gorgeous with his mile-wide shoulders and that way of looking at her that threatened to make her lose her good sense and contemplate ridiculous things such as jumping up and kissing him.

That was not good. Even if the thoughts of kissing him were just that…thoughts. And that's exactly how they would remain—rogue thoughts forever banished to the dark corner of her mind.

Alex Lejardin was of no interest to her beyond being Liam's father because he'd been intimate with her sister. She still didn't know his side of the story…other than that they'd had a child, and that was more than enough information to blind her to his green eyes and great smile.

Even so, as he raised his glass to hers, she heard herself uttering, "Good. I'm glad you can come."

The server brought their food, and they made polite conversation as they ate. After the dishes were cleared, Alex looked at her for a long moment, his face serious.

The light that had shown in his eyes earlier as they talked about the Bundy was gone, replaced by something more solemn.

"So, you're leaving tomorrow," he said, settling back in his chair.

She nodded, grounded by that jolt of reality. "Yes, we are. I can't believe we've been away for three weeks. It's gone by so fast."

"I'm glad it's been a good trip." He absently fingered a coffee spoon that remained on the table, moving it back and forth in a contemplative gesture.

"I'm very grateful to you for bringing my son to me, Julianne. If not for you, I would've lost even more time with him. I might have never known about him at all."

Yes. His tone was definitely too serious.

She had a distinct feeling the flute wasn't the real surprise?

She placed her hands neatly in her lap, one on top of the other, a calming counter to the jarring turn she feared this conversation was about to take.

"I'm glad everything worked out," she said. "I was so nervous coming to your office that first day. Especially since I thought you'd chosen to not be part of Liam's life."

Alex remained quiet for a long moment. The sounds of the busy restaurant—the chatter and clatter of cutlery on china echoing in the void between them.

"There are some things we need to talk about before you go home," Alex said. "Arrangements concerning Liam."

Julianne laced her fingers together tightly,

willing herself not to fidget. Just because he was watching his spoon handle slip back and forth on the table and not looking her in the eyes didn't mean he was going to deliver bad news.

"I told you a little about my family yesterday," he said. "That my brother is married to the queen of St. Michel. So even though Liam is not in line for the throne, he's still related to the royal family."

Julianne nodded, holding her breath because she could tell by the way he paused that there was definitely something more. An *"and..."* waiting in the wings.

"And...I know I haven't spoken much about my job with iWITNESS, but it's a bit dangerous. Not in the same nature that Marissa's job was dangerous. Still, what I do can have serious consequences for some people. People who have no qualms about killing others who get in their way."

What?

His words hit like a white-hot electric jolt.

He picked this moment to lift his lashes and look her in the eyes. The torment she saw in his face caused panic the likes of which she'd never known to hatch in her belly and start clawing its way out.

"Julianne, what I'm getting at is...Liam is a

prime target for retribution. And you are, too, if he lives with you—"

"Don't be ridiculous," she said. "Who would hurt a baby?"

"Sadly, many of the people my organization opposes. Liam needs to be somewhere safe—"

"Are you suggesting I leave Liam with you? I won't give him up. He's all the family I have left. I may not be his biological mother, I've been his only mother for the past three months, and I'll be damned if I'm going to let a man who hasn't even known him forty-eight hours take him away from me."

Alex opened his mouth the speak, but she didn't want to hear what he had to say.

"Do you really expect me to believe that safety is an issue? If so, how can you, as a single father protect him—no, not just *protect* him, how can you raise him, give him the kind of life he deserves while you keep a job that gains you enemies around the world?"

Her foot kicked the edge of the flute case, and she was struck with the urge to give it back to Alex. She'd given him too much credit. The only reason he'd purchased that flute was because he thought it would butter her up.

A flute in exchange for her baby?

Was he crazy? Using some cockamamy story about national security to frighten her into leaving Liam.

"Look, I'm sorry you don't believe me. I know this sounds unreal, but it is very real and you have to understand that. Remember the men you saw in the park? The ones you thought were following us down Boulevard St. Michel? They *were* indeed following us. I hired them to do just that. So, what I'm trying to help you understand is because of both iWITNESS and St. Michel's Secret Service, I have access to state-of-the-art security measures. But only if Liam stays here—or more precisely, in St. Michel."

"No!"

Several people turned and looked at them.

Alex leaned in. "You're welcome to come with him." He spoke in hushed tones, his voice barely above a whisper.

Because she didn't want others eavesdropping on their conversation, she lowered her tone, too. "We can't stay, Alex. We can't just unpack our suitcases and take an extended vacation. Liam and I have a life in Washington. That's our home. I have a job. That's where we belong."

He nodded. "Yes, that is where your life is. I

assumed as much. But I had to make the offer for my son's sake. I know he is attached to you."

Dear God, what have I done by involving Alex in Liam's life? She'd only meant to introduce an uninterested man to his lovable little boy—to make life better for Liam. To ensure he'd always have enough to cover health care and schooling, college even. She never dreamed the Alex that her sister had described would suggest Liam stay with him permanently. That he'd try to take Liam away from her.

She especially hadn't meant to put her baby in harm's way—if the unbelievable scare tactics Alex was using were even true.

"We don't have to come to any conclusions right this minute," Alex said. "However, this is something we need to iron out before you leave Paris tomorrow."

"Sorry, but I won't be willing to give up Liam tomorrow, either."

For once in her life, Julianne did something spontaneous. She pushed her chair away from the table, grabbed her purse and stormed out of the café.

Chapter Five

Alex found his seat in the balcony of the theater. Even though the Continental Symphony Orchestra was a small orchestra, he wanted to be sure he had the best vantage point to see Julianne as she played.

Alex had seen enough orchestra performances to know that as a flutist, Julianne would be seated in the row behind the strings, hidden by her colleagues. So, he'd exchanged the orchestra-level ticket she'd given him for a seat in the balcony.

As he settled in, other patrons began to file into the hall and the musicians began to take their seats on stage, arranging music stands and warming up with scales and various tuning exercises. Alex's gaze immediately snapped to Julianne when she appeared from the wings as if he'd sensed her. Her hair was pulled back into a twist, making her neck look slender and elegant. She moved gracefully to her place, the silver of her flute brilliant against the plain black of her long dress. She settled herself on the edge of her seat, very much in the manner she had that first day in his office, and began the process of readying herself to play.

It was a fascinating glimpse into the world of the classical musician. Into Julianne's world. Though Alex had witnessed this pre-concert buzz numerous times before with different ensembles, actually knowing someone in the orchestra made him see it with new eyes.

Her flute's trill rose above the cacophony of the string and various wind instruments. She went into a series of scales played at a dizzying speed with deft precision.

And this is only her warm-up.

Julianne, like most of the musicians, kept to herself—in a sort of musical zone, it seemed. Cloaked in her typical cool aura, she didn't seem to be bringing any of the upset from today's lunch with her on stage.

Of course not. She is a professional.

Still, he was sorry he'd been forced to drop that unfortunate bomb on her so close to performance time. But there wasn't any other opportunity to talk to her. He'd known she'd need a period of time to digest everything. Once she'd had time to put everything into perspective, they would discuss what would happen next: whether she would send Liam to St. Michel alone or if she would to come with him. The only absolute was that Liam would be going to St. Michel.

Alex's heart felt leaden in his chest, because he knew she probably wasn't any happier now than when she'd left him at the restaurant this afternoon.

She'd set the Bundy flute case on the table.

"Thank you, but I have to turn down your donation because it feels as if you're asking me to exchange *my child* for a used flute."

"Julianne, don't be ridiculous. I'm not trying to bribe or otherwise entice you to exchange *your nephew*. Don't make a rash decision about the boy's safety."

He could see his words weren't winning her over so he changed tactics.

"You said yourself that one of your students could greatly benefit from this flute. In a similar way, Liam needs you to keep an open mind for his well-being."

The way she glared at him made it clear she didn't appreciate the analogy.

"How can you even lump the two into the same category? They're not even remotely similar."

It was a no-win situation. Of course the two were not even in the same category. The flute was junk; Liam was priceless. And that was exactly why he couldn't take any chances with his safety, even if the thought of separating Julianne and Liam killed him.

"Julianne, please be reasonable. Think about the implications of taking Liam back to Washington. Are you really willing to put him in harm's way?"

"Harm's way? I have a hard time believing that a boy you didn't even know existed forty-eight hours ago could be used as a pawn."

She'd been impervious to his words. He'd pushed the flute toward her anyway as she stood to leave.

She glanced down at it and then her blue eyes flashed angrily at him.

"You know what the worst part is, Alex? You want to ship him off, put him in cold storage. What kind of life is that for a little boy? You don't love him. You don't even know him. How can you know what's best for him? But I do. That's why Liam and I are going home tomorrow." She gestured towards the door as if it were the way back to the States. "Please forget you ever met me. You don't have to send money. Not a dime. Then there will be no trail for the bad guys to follow. We'll go so quietly that nobody will even know we were here."

She turned around and walked away before he could answer, leaving him stuck between this rock of reason and the very hard place of knowing what had to be done.

He did love Liam.

He had since the instant he'd seen the boy.

The St. Michel Secret Service men who were now assigned to Liam had reported that Liam was in the building with Anita, the woman who cared for him while Julianne worked. The bodyguards were backstage discreetly watching over the boy. Alex had told them to "blend in" with the backstage crew so as not to alarm Anita. The bodyguards said the babysitter seemed unaware of their presence. Case in point as to why Liam needed professional security.

Giving Anita credit, there was no reason that she'd think Liam needed security—and the best case situation would be that he never would. His bodyguards would remain "off stage" in Liam's life and the boy would live a normal life. He wouldn't live in "cold storage," as Julianne had described it. But even the smallest chance of danger was too much to risk. So, Alex would proceed with his plan.

The auditorium had filled. The lights were dimmed and the concertmaster took his place by the podium to tune the orchestra. Alex watched Julianne with her good posture and gaze on the violinist.

She obviously had her game face on, Alex mused and that was proof that she was a sensible woman. In time, he hoped she would understand that moving Liam to St. Michel was the best thing for the boy. He wasn't doing it to hurt her.

That was the last thing he wanted to do, and tonight after the concert, he intended to make sure she knew that.

How hard could it be to convince a sensible woman like Julianne?

Tonight was the first time Julianne had ever played a concert on autopilot. As she walked off stage, she realized she'd never been so relieved for a program to be over.

She always put her head and heart into her work.

But it was difficult tonight after being blindsided by Alex's announcement at lunch.

As she'd taken the stage tonight, she'd wondered if Alex had come to the performance or if he'd decided to skip it because they'd not parted on very good terms. Although she didn't know exactly where his seat was located, she had a general idea, and she hadn't seen him while the house lights were up. But once the auditorium started filling up, he could've easily slipped in unnoticed. If she'd been thinking straight she would've had the theater's security bar him from the building. A good thought in theory, because Alex was so wrapped up in security measures. Alas, it was logistically impossible because she didn't have the means to cancel his ticket.

She should've stuck to the original plan of leaving his ticket at will call rather than giving it to him earlier today.

To think at one point she'd actually wanted him there. She'd even imagined he'd been flirting with her, which she now knew was ridiculous.

Live and learn. She'd conveniently forgotten that daring Marissa was his type, not conventional Julianne.

She hurried through the backstage area to the green room where Anita was sitting with Liam.

The orchestra's executive director had asked everyone to gather there for a short meeting before the evening's dismissal.

Julianne was eager to see her baby before the meeting started. All night, she'd been wrestling with the gut-wrenching fear that Alex might find some way to take Liam while she was on stage. But she had a show to perform. Her colleagues were counting on her.

She was a professional, so she filed the fear in the same compartment in the back of her mind where she filed Alex's unlikely claims that a terrorist group might try to harm Liam. Still, her hand shook as she reached for the green room's door and jerked it open.

Relief washed over her when she saw her baby sound asleep in his travel crib. Anita sat in a nearby chair.

"Hi," she said to Anita. "How was everything?"

"He was a perfect angel. You all sounded great out there."

The scene was so reassuring—so normal—it made everything that had happened earlier that day seem no more substantial than a bad dream she'd just woken from.

A bad dream that had plagued her all day,

even after Julianne had had a chance to take a step back and think about everything Alex said. She'd seriously considered Alex's assertions. For a moment, she'd let herself go there, to the scary place of Alex's kidnapping monsters, but she kept coming back to the fact that Marissa hadn't been afraid that anything would happen to Liam—and Marissa had lived with her baby on the outskirts of hell.

If Marissa had believed Liam was safe in Afghanistan of all places, unguarded by anyone other than a babysitter, then Julianne had to believe that her sister would've thought the safe little life Julianne and Liam led in the States was perfectly fine.

Knowing that Alex's brother had married royalty, Marissa hadn't tried to hide the identity of Liam's father—good grief, she'd even named Alex on the birth certificate. So it wasn't as if Liam's paternity was a big secret—yet Marissa hadn't felt the need to surround her son with Secret Service agents. Yes, it all made sense now. She'd wanted him to live a normal, ordinary life: the kind of life Julianne was giving him; one where he could run and play and go to school and make friends like any other normal, ordinary child.

That's why she'd named Julianne his guardian.

She certainly hadn't asked that the boy be sent to live with his father or his extended royal family.

Because of Marissa's choice, Julianne believed that Marissa would've wanted for Liam exactly the kind of life Julianne was giving him.

So she would honor her sister's wishes.

That's why she decided she couldn't allow Alex to secrete the boy away to St. Michel.

Even after rationally coming to this conclusion, Julianne still had to ask herself why Alex had been so dramatic about the situation. Was it because he wanted custody of his son? Because he didn't necessarily want custody, but he didn't want there to be an ocean between them?

Or maybe he wanted the fact that he had a child kept on the down low. If he sent Liam to St. Michel he'd be out of the way. No one else would ever know that Alex Lejardin ever had a son. Whether he was in the market for hot girlfriends or a prestigious wife, a baby by another woman could be a hindrance.

Suddenly Julianne was wondering if that might not have been the reason he abandoned her sister when she was pregnant. A baby didn't fit in with his plans. Not then, and not now.

Her cell phone vibrated in the pocket of her skirt. Since Liam had come to live with her she always carried her phone with her everywhere— even on stage. Just in case. Thank goodness there had never been any emergencies.

Alex Lejardin's name registered on the phone's display. Julianne sent the call to voice mail. The moment the phone registered the message, she dialed her voice mailbox.

"Hello, Julianne, it was a fabulous concert this evening. I wanted to come backstage and congratulate you myself, but the restaurant will be a better place to meet. I know you were unhappy with me earlier today, but I also know that you're a reasonable woman. In that vein, I look forward to having dinner with you tonight so that we can iron out the details. I'll see you at the Bistro Garnier on the Rue des Capucines. I look forward to having this settled between us."

She was debating whether to call him back when Hal Ford, the orchestra's executive director, called the meeting to order.

"First, I want to congratulate everyone on a fabulous end to a fabulous tour. Three weeks on the road, and I know that everyone is looking forward to getting home. You should have your tickets and return flight information. If you have any questions, please see me.

"I can't say enough good about the performances.

We've gotten rave reviews throughout Europe. I'm so glad we can leave on such a stellar note. And that brings me to the main reason I've gathered everyone together tonight."

The room was so silent that you could have heard the proverbial crickets chirping if not for the sudden, weighty shift in air.

"It gives me great pain to announce that this was the last performance for the Continental Symphony Orchestra." A collective gasp sounded and murmuring rippled through the room.

"Unfortunately," Hal continued, "the sponsor we were negotiating with has decided to take funding in a different direction. That, I'm afraid, leaves us no choice but to disband. I know this must come as a great shock to most of you."

Most, but not all.

A group of astute "old-timers," who had played together in orchestras of many incarnations, had already caught wind that something like this might happen and had been talking about reorganizing. They'd included Julianne in those talks. Even though they knew something like this was coming down the pike, they'd been hoping to get a little mileage out of the European tour.

Nothing definite had been put together yet but they'd be able to reorganize in a matter of months.

If not for Liam, Julianne would have considered this the exciting start to a new venture. But all she could think, as she handed Liam to Anita and began folding his crib and gathering his gear, was that she was unemployed, perhaps for months. Perhaps even longer.

And that put her in a very vulnerable position where Alex Lejardin was concerned.

Chapter Six

They were leaving tonight. They wouldn't wait to travel with the group tomorrow. It was a snap decision that came to Julianne as soon as she and Liam left the Opéra Garnier and were in a cab on their way back to the hotel.

It was only a matter of time before Alex found out that the orchestra had folded and would be able to use it against her. Her sudden unemployment fueled an urgency to get Liam out of Paris and home where he belonged.

Over the years, she'd learned to always trust her gut, and right now it was screaming for her to take Liam and leave.

By no means was she planning on cutting Alex out of Liam's life. She wanted him to have a relationship with his father. But it had become distressingly obvious today that she better be sure of her legal rights before Alex whisked Liam away to a foreign country, where she might not have any legal standing.

She couldn't risk never seeing her baby again.

The first thing she'd do once she got home was hire an attorney. She'd find a way to afford it— even if she had to take a job flipping burgers. It would be honest work. Honest money. And if that's what it took to support her child, that's what she'd do until the orchestra reorganized and got back on solid footing.

There was *always* a way.

She just had to remember that when hope started slipping.

By the time the cab reached the hotel, Julianne had called the airlines and rebooked Liam and herself on a 3:00 a.m. flight out of Charles de Gaulle. The flight-change fees were hefty, but she couldn't afford *not* to do it.

It was close to 11:00 p.m. by the time they got back to the hotel. She'd have just enough time to get up to the room, pack their things and get to the airport in time for the international fight. The timing would work nicely because Liam was sound asleep. More importantly, Alex would still be waiting at the restaurant for her while she and Liam were en route to de Gaulle. By the time he realized what had happened, she and Liam would be somewhere over the Atlantic Ocean. Safe. Probably closer to home than here.

As Julianne packed, she went over her mental checklist. She had to let the others know. She couldn't just not show up at the airport tomorrow when the orchestra members would be expecting her. She decided she'd leave a note at the front desk to be given to Anita upon checkout. In the note, she'd ask Anita to explain to the group that she and Liam had gone on ahead and—

A knock on the door startled her from her planning, sending volts of fear searing through her. She glanced at Liam, who was sleeping soundly in his port-a-crib, then back at the door.

Oh, God.

The walk to the door seemed to take forever. Her limbs were heavy, like the sluggishness in dreams where you're running from something horrible and your legs can't carry you away fast enough. She took a deep breath before she looked out the peephole.

It was worse than she feared. Not only was Alex standing there, he'd brought several men with him.

Sheer black fear knotted inside her and her heart slammed against her breastbone.

Dear God, there was no way out.

Julianne was trying to run.

Although Alex didn't want to believe she'd do such a thing, another part of him chastised himself for not anticipating it.

He wasn't angry with her. Even though they were on different sides of this battle. He understood. He'd learned from the Secret Service agents stationed at the theater that the orchestra members had received word that the group was officially disbanded.

She'd panicked, he imagined. Fight or flight. If he'd been in her shoes, he might have fled, too. He was glad they'd gotten here before she'd left.

As he stood in the dimly lit hotel hall, surrounded by St. Michel Secret Service agents and hotel security, he knocked lightly once again.

"Julianne, it's Alex. Please open the door."

His request was met with silence.

Secret Service had flagged her name with the airlines. When she tried to switch flights, officials had been alerted immediately. The agents had been doing their jobs—and damned well.

"Julianne, hotel security and the Secret Service are here with me. If you won't open the door, they will unlock it."

He shook his head regretfully. This wasn't the way he wanted things to go. He made sure he kept the knocking to a low rap—loud enough for her to hear it, but civilized enough so that it didn't scare Liam or cause a scene that attracted onlookers. Luckily, the hotel hallway was empty except for them. For now, at least. There were only twelve rooms on the floor—six across from each other, situated in a wide hallway. He needed this to be resolved as quickly and quietly as possible.

It had to be frightening enough for her to be in there alone with a small child, let alone knowing there was a bunch of men outside, demanding she open the door. Frankly, he didn't blame her if she didn't obey.

Of course, that would mean that security would unlock it with a master key.

"Julianne, please."

Alex stared at the deep red carpet, straining his ears, hoping to hear her say something in response, anything to indicate that she was willing to comply.

The lead hotel security guard, a tall, wiry man, put his hand up to the Bluetooth radio set on his left ear. "Apparently, she called the front desk to ask for security to be sent to her room," he told them. "They told her that security was already there and asked her to open the door."

As if the security guard had uttered the magic words, the hotel room door creaked opened a crack.

"Alex," she said, "why are you doing this? You must have some idea of how much it will upset Liam."

Julianne still had the security latch on the door so that it couldn't be opened from the outside without considerable force, although there were ways around that contraption, ways that weren't cordial or quiet, but ways in, nonetheless.

Alex had made it clear to the hotel's security team that this was a nonviolent intervention. It would remain so, unless he instructed otherwise.

"I'm very sorry," he said to Julianne, looking her straight in the eye she used to peep out the door crack. And truly he was. These certainly weren't the conditions under which he'd hoped and imagined he'd find himself in a hotel with this woman. "Why did you decide to leave Paris early? And without telling me?"

"Because I wanted to avoid exactly this situation." She said. "How did you find out I was leaving?"

Even through the slit in the door, he could see the stress in her eyes. "The Secret Service was alerted when you changed your flight. I can only assume that you weren't aware that Paris authorities recognize St. Michel law. They won't let you take Liam out of the country."

"I want to talk to someone at the U.S. Embassy," she hissed.

"Julianne, it won't matter. My name is on Liam's birth certificate. I am his father. I want him to stay. I am inviting you to stay with him. I'm not trying to take him away from you. But for this to work out, you have to open the door."

She hesitated, and he could see the tears flowing down her cheeks. He had such an urge to reach out and wipe them away, to gather her in his arms and let her cry on his shoulder. It killed him to think that he was the cause of those tears. But this stubborn woman had given him no alternative.

He stepped closer to the door, leaned his head against the jamb so that the only thing separating them was the door's small opening. Surprisingly, she didn't move away.

"I'm sorry." His voice was as quiet. "I know

it must look ominous with all these men outside
your door, but I won't let anything bad happen to
you. They're not going to arrest you or harm you
or even separate you from Liam. You are welcome
to go anywhere he goes. I want you to come with
us. I just need you to let me in."

He didn't know where the words came from—
some untapped place in his heart he never knew existed. And why? Because she was good for Liam?
Because maybe in some way he'd never expected
or experienced, she might be good for him, too?

She was sobbing now, her head against the door
frame. He could feel the warmth of her sweet breath
on his lips. He let her cry for a moment, until her
sobs had subsided. Then he reached through the
crack in the door and wiped away a meandering
tear.

"Ask them to leave and I'll let you in, Alex. Only
you."

Without hesitation, he turned to his colleagues.
"Could you give us a moment?"

There was some hesitancy, some murmured dis-
cussion about whether this was a prudent move.
But finally security dispersed, covering all viable
exits. After all, she was on the sixth floor. There
were no balconies and no fire escapes in the room.
The only way she was getting out was through

a hotel door. Even though she was stubborn and determined and fiercely protective of Liam, Alex knew Julianne wasn't stupid.

When the others had gone and it was just Alex standing by himself, the door clicked shut. He heard the rasp of metal on metal as she released the security latch and opened the door to let him in.

Chapter Seven

Trapped.

That's how Julianne had felt as Alex and his band of secret service agents had shepherded Liam and her aboard a St. Michel state jet.

Trapped and transported to the small principality at Alex's command.

Like a fox that had been outsmarted, cornered and caught, she'd had no choice but to surrender after Alex had allowed her to contact the U.S. Embassy in Paris.

After some confusion, a legal representative from the Embassy had confirmed the truth of Alex's assertions. Since Alex was named Liam's father on the child's birth certificate, Alex's parental rights outranked hers as appointed guardian.

Alex was the one who had the definitive say as to where Liam would live, and Alex had decreed that he and the boy were going to St. Michel.

"You're invited to join us," he'd assured her.

For the past twenty-four hours she'd hated him for it. For essentially ripping the child from her life and making her nothing more than an invited guest who had no choice but to accept the precarious invitation.

She detested Alex Lejardin for forcing her to come to St. Michel. She was prepared to detest everything about the godforsaken…and purportedly unbelievably beautiful place he was taking her to.

But the conscientious objector in her was short-lived.

Once they boarded the plane bound for Alex's home and family, she'd managed to put a cap on her anger. She certainly wasn't going to cause a scene that would upset Liam. He was a smart little guy. He sensed when she was upset. They were so close that often his moods mirrored hers.

Having a baby in her life had been a never-ending lesson in humility. For Liam's sake, as well as her own, she'd learned to defuse stress and anger, keeping him away from negative emotions as much as possible.

This unexpected sojourn was proving to be one of the toughest tests of her mettle she'd ever experienced.

She had no choice—even if she didn't like the situation, she was going to make the best of it and regroup once she had a chance to seek legal counsel.

Sometime during the flight to St. Michel, somewhere over the ocean, her anger faded away. She realized that once her feet were firmly planted on St. Michel soil.

It wasn't the luxury of the private jet that couriered her there that appeased her—if anything, that would've added to her displeasure. There were few things she disliked more than someone with money riding roughshod over those who couldn't fight on the same battlefield. As an artist, she'd witnessed it plenty of times with patrons whose philosophy was *my way or the highway*.

Nor was it the first-class treatment she received during the short flight from Paris.

The tipping point came in the tender way Alex had treated not only Liam, but also her.

She'd expected him to be angry.

He wasn't.

She'd expected him to at least act sullen or superior.

He'd been the opposite: open and willing to talk; forthright about explaining why he'd had to do what he'd done; willing to hear Julianne out and let her have a say in certain options involving Liam.

He'd even taken care to inform her colleagues of her "change of plans" and ensured that they had been given her contact information.

No wonder her sister had fallen in love with him. Julianne was beginning to understand the effect he could have on women. Maybe her change of heart was caused by something he'd slipped into the sparkling water she'd sipped aboard the jet.

No, she'd experienced the pull of Alex Lejardin before he'd leveled her with the news that he was taking Liam to St. Michel.

If she thought too hard about the effect he seemed to have on her, or even the fact that she still found him attractive in the midst of this friendly kidnapping, she felt simply ridiculous.

So she decided not to think about it, not to think about him that way.

When they exited the plane in St. Michel, a black stretch limousine waited on the airfield. Julianne hugged Liam a little tighter and Alex carried the boy's car seat as they crossed the tarmac toward the limo.

"My brother and sister-in-law sent a car."

Very thoughtful of the queen and prince consort.

The uniformed driver greeted them, opened the door and set to work installing Liam's seat on the rear-facing seat of the limo.

The sun shone in the sky but while it was warmer here than in Paris, there was still a chill in the air.

"It's beautiful here," Julianne said. "I could see that as we flew in, but I thought it would be more tropical."

"No, actually, St. Michel is located roughly the same latitude as Boston. But it's warmer here because the Alps shield it from icy winter winds. It's relative. Compared to Boston, fifty-five degrees might seem tropical this time of year."

"Well, I won't expect to spend a lot of time on the beach, then."

"You can spend as much time as you'd like at the beach. But I must warn you, this is the wet season. It rains several times a week."

They stood in silence for a few moments waiting for the driver to finish.

"Here's a bit of trivia for you," Alex said. "St.

Michel used to be a winter retreat for Britain's rich and famous. Now, the big season is in the summer. Even if the weather is a little cooler now, at least you can enjoy it without the traffic jams and other hassles of summer tourism."

"Are you always Mr. Brightside?" Julianne asked.

"Are you always the cynic?" A mischievous glint danced in his eyes.

She smiled at him. "Touché."

"After you," Alex took Liam from her and with his free hand he took hold of Julianne's arm to steady her as she climbed into the car. She settled herself on the seat across from where the driver had installed Liam's infant seat. Alex handed the boy to her and she strapped him in. By the time she'd finished, Alex was sitting beside her and the driver had closed the door.

Chauffeured limos and private planes.

It was all a little surreal. She certainly wasn't used to being on this side of luxury. She was starting to realize that here, she would probably see a completely different side of Alex.

A side that Marissa had never spoken of. All her sister had said was that Alex was a good-looking lawyer.

Julianne's gaze drifted to the center of the

car's bar area where an ice bucket with a bottle of champagne sat chilling. Alex extracted it from the bucket, picked up the cloth napkin that was laid out beside it and wiped the water from the bottle.

"Ah, look, Krug Clos du Mesnil." As the words rolled off Alex's tongue, his French accent was more pronounced. Even so, he said the name of the champagne—one she'd never heard of—as if it were as common as Korbel.

"Very nice," he said. "It's my brother's favorite nectar."

Alex dislodged the cork and poured two glasses, handing one to Julianne.

"Welcome to St. Michel."

In somewhat of a daze, she found herself clinking glasses with Alex. "Thank you."

They sipped their drinks as Liam cooed softly in his seat. He'd slept most of the way, after having a breakfast of cereal and a banana on the plane. He seemed perfectly content riding in his little seat. A good traveler, Julianne thought as she contemplated him over the top of her glass. Along for the ride.

So was she, apparently. At least for the time being. Until she could get settled and figure out what she was doing next.

She sat back in her seat and turned her attention

out the window, catching her first glimpse of this place that might very well be Liam's new home.

The enormity of the thought made her shudder.

"So, where are we going?" she asked.

"We're staying at the Palais de St. Michel. Luc and Sophie have invited us to stay as long as we like."

"In other words, if Liam and I want to leave in two or three days, we're free to go?"

He smiled ruefully. "Not exactly."

What he wasn't saying was that *she* was free to go anytime she wanted to leave. But Liam was not.

"I just don't want to impose on your family's hospitality."

"That's hardly possible. The Palais has 210 bedrooms and 75 bathrooms. Not to mention the 95 offices and staterooms. The place is like a small city. We could go weeks without running into each other."

"So, you could hold us prisoner here and no one would be the wiser?"

"No one except for the hundreds of employees who work at the palace, but they're paid well enough that they'll keep my secret." Julianne could hear the laughter under his statement.

He touched her arm and his shoulder pressed into her as he leaned forward and gestured out the window toward a harbor brimming with yachts. "That's the St. Michel Marina. I keep my boat docked there. I don't own property in St. Michel, but I have a boat. Maybe tomorrow we can take it out for a sail?"

"Those are some pretty big boats," Julianne said, completely and utterly aware of the heat of Alex's arm. Even after he settled back into his seat, he was still sitting so close that his arm was pressed against hers.

"Mine is modest compared to some of the boats kept there. Are you familiar with Stavros Andros, the Greek shipping magnate?"

Julianne nodded.

"His old yacht *Poseidon V* is still housed there. After Stavros died, the son of St. Michel's former minister of finance purchased it, but both he and his father are in jail for treason, murder and various other charges."

"Is that a warning?"

The way he was looking at her ignited a flush that started at the base of her neck and crept upward.

"Yes, that is the fate of troublesome guests."

"Nice."

"Ah, we're here." Alex pushed the button that lowered the privacy panel between them and the driver. "Excuse me, please circle around to the front of the castle so that the *mademoiselle* can have a good view of it before you pass through the security gates."

"Certainly," the driver said in accented English.

Alex settled back, his arm, once again resting against hers. "So here's your history lesson for the day. Are you ready?"

She nodded looking in wonder as they rounded a corner and a grand palace appeared in full view, as stately and splendid as a picture that might appear in a book called *Magnificent Castles of the World*.

"The Palais de St. Michel was built in the thirteenth century. The exterior of the castle still resembles the original thirteenth-century fortress, but the inside has been renovated and updated with the most modern of security and conveniences."

"Which is the reason we're here," she quipped. "For the modern security and conveniences."

"You catch on fast."

There was that smile that always made her stomach do a triple gainer. She sat forward in her seat ignoring the way her body betrayed her. Instead, she let the thought that *this* was where they were going to stay steal her breath away. In the five years she'd lived in Washington, D.C., she'd never been inside the White House. She'd walked past it many times, but she'd always been too busy to plan ahead and make a reservation for a tour. Each time she passed by, she'd look at it wistfully and promise herself that someday she'd go inside. *Someday...*

The Palais de St. Michel had the same effect.

Only this time she didn't have to stand outside the gates dreaming of what it would be like inside.

In a matter of minutes she'd be in.

"Is the castle open for public tours?" she asked.

"The staterooms are open during summer, and tours are almost always booked to capacity."

"That's a lot of people visiting each year," she said.

As they continued to drive, Alex pointed at an expanse of manicured lawn. "See that?"

She nodded.

"Here's a fact that I think you'll find interesting: For the past one hundred years, the palace courtyard has been the setting for concerts given by the St. Michel National Orchestra. I'll check when the season begins."

Season? He was talking in seasons, and she wasn't sure how long she'd be there. The thought threatened to rob a little bit of the magic from the moment.

"But the Palais de St. Michel isn't simply a tourist attraction and museum," he continued. "It's also a fully working palace and the government headquarters. My brother and sister-in-law are involved with the day-to-day running of St. Michel. Basically, running the country is my sister-in-law's family business."

He smiled, which made his eyes crinkle at the corners in a way that caused Julianne's gaze to linger and her belly to flutter again.

The car continued its circle around the palace, causing them to list to the left and his shoulder to press into hers a bit more. For a moment, Julianne gave in to the gravity that made his body lean into hers and she lost herself in the masculine feel of him.

When the car straightened, neither of them reclaimed their personal space. And for just a moment, she wondered what the rest of his body would feel like pressed against hers.

She trained her gaze out the window because her cheeks were flaming and she couldn't look at him.

As they completed the circle around the palace, she watched, captivated, as the majestic building passed outside the window, a stately scene of white stone set against the azure sky.

Wow, was she ever out of her league.

Suddenly she felt very small and a travel-weary exhaustion seeped into her bones. The initial adrenaline rush that had first presented itself as excitement faded into a strange sort of homesickness that manifested in the very center of her soul.

When they reached the palace's unassuming back security entrance, armed sentries saluted as the limo proceeded through a series of gates.

There was no pretense of fairy-tale castles back here. This was serious business.

She leaned away from Alex's hard body and reclaimed her personal space.

He seemed to understand because he respected the distance she'd put between them.

Once inside, the limo stopped in front of a set of steel doors that opened automatically. The car crept into the gaping mouth of the garage area. When the doors closed behind them, it was as if they were swallowed whole. Julianne took Liam out of his seat as a uniformed attendant opened the car door. He ushered them out of the limo and into an elevator, which carried them into the bowels of the castle to the living quarters—a wing never open to the public.

Julianne was about to meet her first—and quite possibly her last—monarch. She swallowed her nerves and put on her best face for Liam's sake.

"Let's go meet your aunt, sweetie."

Chapter Eight

Alex could tell that Julianne was taken aback by the world he'd swept her into. To make her more comfortable, as the palace elevator carried them to their floor, he explained what was happening.

"The staff have been told only that the prince's brother and his guests would arrive today," he said. "They weren't given details about Liam. It's probably best that we don't make announcements—even to the staff. Don't get me wrong, Liam's important, but the less fanfare the better. Do you agree?"

Julianne bit her bottom lip for a moment, before answering.

"I was the one who wanted to go quietly back

to Washington and resume life as normal. So, yes, I agree. The less fanfare the better."

There was an edge to her voice that sometimes made it seem as if she were baiting him. His gaze fell to her lips. She had a smart mouth to go along with her brains, beauty and talent. He liked it and respected her for it.

She challenged him, not content to take everything at face value. Above all, he admired her because she put Liam first. Bringing the baby to St. Michel was hard on her. It was disruptive and unfair, but it was necessary. She was a trouper, doing what was best for the boy.

When the elevator doors opened, two middle-aged women in traditional gray-and-white maid uniforms stood at the ready. Alex didn't recognize them. Not that he was a frequent guest. In fact, he hadn't been here since Luc and Sophie's wedding more than a year ago.

"*Monsieur, mademoiselle,* we welcome you to the Palais de St. Michel." They curtsied.

"I am Isobel," said the taller of the two. "This is Aimée. We are at your service."

Alex gestured for Julianne to precede him as they followed the attendants down the long hallway—the tap-tap-tap of four pairs of shoes resonating on the parquet floors. Stopping in front of a set of white double doors trimmed in ornate gilded scrollwork, Isobel opened them with a flourish.

"This suite is for the *mademoiselle* and the baby." She gestured inside. "*Monsieur* will be right next door."

Aimée opened the doors to Alex's room in similar fashion, but she remained silent.

Because Isobel was doing all the talking, Julianne wondered if Aimée spoke English. If not, she seemed to have the drill down.

"You will find your bags inside," Isobel said.

That was fast.

The efficiency conjured notions of secret passageways within the castle's ancient infrastructure.

Or maybe not. Judging by the women's crisp uniforms, Julianne had a hunch that everything around here ran that efficiently.

"Do you require anything now?" Isobel asked.

"Julianne?" Alex deferred to her with his impeccable manners.

"I should be fine. Liam will need an afternoon snack soon."

Isobel smiled. "I believe the chef has instructions on what the boy eats. I will have the kitchen prepare something and send it right up."

And where did they get that list?

"Thank you," Julianne said, wondering what

other bits of information the "palace" knew about them. Even if she didn't have anything to hide, it was a little unnerving that the entire staff of the Palais de St. Michel might know all about her although she was unaware of how they'd come to possess such information.

Was it that easy to gather information?

She shivered, suddenly seeing Alex's concerns about terrorists and kidnappers in a different light.

Big Brother obviously was watching. And she had a hunch it wasn't simply Alex's big brother, Luc. If the omniscient Big Brother was a bully, there was no telling what he might do.

Okay, she got it.

But that didn't mean she had to like it.

Liam cooed and pointed to a painting of an angel hanging in the hallway. Julianne was glad to have something to shift her focus.

"Pretty," she answered.

Pretty was an understatement. This hall was like a museum wing with its gilded-framed paintings, sculptures and vases on pedestals. She made sure she kept at least an arm's length away from anything breakable so that Liam wouldn't be tempted to touch.

"*Monsieur,* may I get you anything?" Isobel asked.

"No, thank you. I believe I have everything I need." Alex's gaze stayed on Julianne and Liam.

Isobel made a gesture that was more than a nod but not quite a full-fledged bow. "This evening, you will be dining with Her Majesty and Prince Luc. Dinner will be served in their apartment at seven-thirty. In the meantime, I hope you will find your accommodations to your satisfaction. If not, do not hesitate to ring."

"Thank you." Alex's voice was politely dismissive, a clue that he was comfortable dealing with the *help*. With another nod/bow, Isobel and Aimée turned and left, leaving Alex and Julianne alone in the fancy hallway.

They stood a moment, facing each other, both in front of their respective suite doors.

"They should have a crib set up and ready for Liam," Alex said. "Do you need help?"

She glanced inside, expecting to see beds in a room, hotel-room fashion, but saw instead that the doors opened into a living room.

"I'm sure everything is fine," she said. "So…I'll see you later?"

"Yes, later."

He turned to enter his room.

"Will you get us for dinner?" The words slipped out of her mouth before she could stop them. She hadn't meant to sound quite so needy, but she didn't know where the royal apartment was located. She felt even more foolish when she realized, one second after she'd spoken, that an escort would probably appear at her door to guide her. The folks at the Palais de St. Michel seemed to be good at anticipating what guests needed before they knew it themselves.

"Of course," Alex said. "I was planning on it."

"Thanks," she said.

They both lingered.

"Well, I guess I should get him settled. Maybe he'll sleep a bit before his snack arrives."

Alex nodded. "Let me know if you need anything."

Her "room" turned out to be a suite considerably larger and nicer than her own apartment in D.C. Two bedrooms, two baths, a living room with a fire burning in the fireplace…a person could definitely get used to this.

So she reminded herself, she'd better not get too comfortable. She had phone calls to make.

Although she could see Alex's point about security, and Alex seemed to be fair and willing to involve her in most of the decisions affecting Liam, she wouldn't be able to relax until after she'd spoken to an attorney.

She wasn't content to take the word of the U.S. Embassy's legal representative. He'd made a snap judgment with St. Michel Secret Service breathing down his neck. She wanted her legal rights defined. Right now everything seemed fine, but who knew what the future might bring? She couldn't stay here forever, and she certainly didn't want to leave without Liam. Not after she'd promised Marissa she'd raise him.

Now that they were on St. Michel soil, in the towers of the royal fortress, she really was at Alex's mercy. If they wanted to take her baby, they could.

Even though she wanted to believe that wouldn't happen, that she'd never have reason to think about legalities, she had to cover all her bases.

After she'd gotten Liam to sleep, she gathered her cell phone, a pen and paper and called Anita Collins to enlist help finding counsel.

Half an hour later, not only had Anita helped her come up with a list of potential attorneys who might be able to help her, but she'd also put Graham on the phone. He had news about the reorganization and was eager for Julianne to get home.

This was good news. If Graham's plan panned out, the orchestra folding might've been a blessing in disguise. The proverbial *when a door closes a window opens* came to mind.

She needed a computer to do some research. Even though there was a nice Mac with tempting Internet service, she decided she'd wait until she could go into town to use a public connection.

Take that, Big Brother.

As if in response, there was a knock at her door. It startled her for a moment, but then she remembered it was probably palace staff with Liam's snack. When she opened the door she was surprised to see Alex standing there holding the beat-up Bundy flute case.

The flute. For her foundation. She'd been too proud, too furious with him yesterday...had it only been yesterday that everything was different?

"You forgot this." He held out the flute to her as if that was really what happened.

"And you brought it to me. You're just thoughtful like that, aren't you?"

He smiled. "It's been said that thoughtfulness is one of my virtues."

"Alex, if you continue to be this *thoughtful,* I simply don't know what I'm going to do with you."

His gaze shifted to her mouth.

"I might be able to make a few suggestions."

She bit the insides of her cheeks. Heat spread like wildfire over her face and she turned away from him, motioning him into the living room.

"Come in."

That was the thing about this maddening man, sometimes—most of the time, in fact—he caught her off guard, upsetting her equilibrium.

Sometimes he was so darn thoughtful that it was hard to think about calling lawyers and playing hardball. But maybe that was his strategy? Subdue her with kindness.

The sobering thought helped the blush pass.

"Thank you for that." She gestured to the flute. "Liam's sleeping, and I was enjoying the fire."

He set the case on the entryway table and followed her into the living room.

The notebook in which she'd jotted notes about lawyers was open and lying on the couch where she'd left it. She promptly closed it and set it on the far side of the large, square granite-topped coffee table as he sat on the couch. She settled herself next to him.

"Were you working?" he asked, looking at the note pad.

She hesitated for a moment, but then in a flash, she decided to be up front with him.

"I'm researching U.S.-based attorneys. I think

you need to know that I still plan on learning what my options are. As you know, I can't stay here forever. And I simply can't imagine being separated from my child."

He nodded, but it wasn't a gesture of agreement. More like an indication of comprehension. "You like to be in charge, don't you?" he asked.

She shrugged. "You say that like it's a bad thing."

"I didn't say it was bad."

"It wasn't so much what you said, as how you said it." She arched a brow. "Do you have a problem with strong women?"

"Of course not."

His prickly response came a little too quickly.

Is that why you left Marissa? The question was poised right on the tip of her tongue, but he spoke first. "It just seems like you always have to drive. Sometimes it might be nice to let go, let someone else take the wheel for a change."

She blinked, unsure of what to say. Truly, she knew that letting go of the reins was a challenge. Being in control was part of who she was.

"I guess I've always been the driver," she said. "Or at least the planner and the one in charge. Marissa was the carefree, happy-go-lucky one."

She held her breath, as if uttering her sister's

name would invite her ghost to wedge its way between Alex and her again.

"Why is that?" he asked.

"Our parents died one month before my eigh-
teenth birthday. Marissa was four years younger
than I was so I had to fight to gain custody of her.
I wasn't going to lose her."

"And you won." Alex did not sound amazed.

"It wasn't easy," Julianne admitted.

"I'm sorry." He touched her arm, lightly. "About
your loss. It must've been a terrible shock and a lot
to bear for someone so young. First, your parents
and then Marissa…"

His eyes held genuine sympathy.

"The past twenty-four hours have felt like
history is repeating itself, Alex. Here I am once
again, fighting for custody of the only family I
have left."

Life had been such a blur over the handful of
months since Liam had come into her life that she
hadn't realized the similarities until now. Hadn't
realized how natural it was for her to fight tooth
and nail for those who belonged to her.

Alex's exhale was sharp, as if her words had
made an impact.

"I'm not trying to take him away from you," he

said. "By now, I'd hoped that was evident." His words were soothing, not defensive.

"Well, yes, but can you understand how strange this feels? We were supposed to be on our way home today. Instead, we're somewhere in the bowels of a castle in a foreign country. Do you see where I'm coming from? I mean what would happen if I took Liam and walked out of here?"

He inclined his head slightly, narrowing his eyes, as if contemplating the question. "You'd probably get lost. The palace is like a maze. One of the more primitive security features. And I'm not exactly keeping you in a dungeon."

She clucked her tongue and gave his leg a light, get-serious push. "Very funny. But I'm serious. I want to know what would happen if I tried to leave?"

His gaze studied her face, making a languid perusal of her features. "You're not a prisoner here, Julianne. Would you like to get out? Perhaps go for a sail on my boat or take a tour of St. Michel?"

That wasn't exactly what she'd meant by *leaving,* and she knew he understood that when he said, "Be patient, Julianne. I'm trying very hard to make this a win-win situation for everyone involved."

She nodded.

"Thank you," he answered. "I still think it might

be a good idea if you got out. The only way you can fully appreciate St. Michel is to see it. I would love to have the honor of being your official tour guide. Do we have a date tomorrow?"

"Gee, I don't know. Let me check my calendar." She paused for a moment. "What do you know? I just happen to be free tomorrow. But first, let's get through dinner tonight with the queen and her prince. They may exile me to the dungeon."

She was trying to be funny, but from the way Alex frowned, she wasn't sure if it translated.

"Sophie and Luc are great people. Give them a chance and I think you'll see that."

Oh. Oops. To her, they were the sovereign rulers, the decision makers, deciders of fate. To Alex, they were simply Luc and Sophie. Oldest brother and sister-in-law.

"Of course. I'm sorry. I'm sure they're *wonderful* people."

And honestly, if they were anything like him, they would be.

"I guess I'm just a little nervous."

"Don't be."

He touched her arm and the heartrending tenderness of his gaze made her achingly aware of how close the two of them were sitting on the couch.

He reached up and traced her lower lip with the

pad of his thumb, and suddenly the air changed, the tenderness was replaced by something electric and dangerous.

"Don't be nervous." He ordered, tenderly.

Her gaze fell to his lips and she wondered how he would taste. A burning crescendo of suppressed desire seared through her, gripping her by surprise. She knew that she was playing with fire…but she just couldn't help it. Didn't want to help it…

The next thing she knew, she was in his arms and his lips were right there, inches from hers.

It started as a whisper of a kiss that made her heart pound and her brain say, *oooh,* as her reason flew out the window.

It began leisurely, slowly, starting with a brush of lips and hints of tongue. As if he were testing the waters to see how she'd react. When she slid her arms around his neck and opened her mouth inviting him in, he turned her so that he could deepen the kiss. Julianne fisted her hands into his hair and pulled their bodies closer.

She'd forgotten how consuming a kiss could be. Alex's hands were on her back and his mouth was on her lips, but her entire body sang. Every sense was heightened as if his touch had awakened the female side of her that had been sleeping for far too long.

Oooh, yes.

She'd forgotten what a kiss from an attractive man could do.

She heard the ragged edge of his breathing just before the blood rushing in her ears. She felt the heat of his hands on her back. He smelled like heaven: a heady mix of soap and a subtle after-shave with grassy notes and something leathery and masculine. Yet despite the intoxicating way he smelled, the way he tasted—of mint and something else that was hard to pin down—nearly made her drunk with pleasure. The two combined were a seductive mix, that teased her senses, making her feel hot and sexy and just a little bit reckless.

Best of all, here in his arms, she didn't feel like she had to *drive.* She wanted to melt into him, let him take charge for a while.

As he tasted and teased, the last bit of reason she possessed took flight with the realization that it had been far too long since a man's touch had made her blood churn and her body long to be fully taken.

She was lost in the feel of him, the smell and taste of him, until something out of place pushed its way into her awareness.

Finally, a low but determined *knock, knock,*

knock on the door pierced her conscious thoughts.

She jumped, dropping her arms from around his neck, pulling away, suddenly desperate to regain her personal space.

Alex froze for a heartbeat. Then he sat back on the couch, looking a little disoriented. They stared at each other for a moment until the next knock began, louder this time.

"That's probably Liam's snack," Julianne murmured.

He let out a long breath and raked a hand through his hair. "I'll get it."

He pushed himself up off the couch and the magnitude of the situation washed over her.

What on earth had she been thinking?

Well, obviously, she hadn't been thinking at all.

She watched his back as he crossed the room toward the door. Those broad shoulders and narrow hips... They were a lethal combination. On a physical level, Julianne couldn't deny she was fiercely attracted to him, and she knew lots of women would be thrilled to change places with her, to find themselves in a storybook castle in the arms of Alex Lejardin.

But what the heck was she doing? She hadn't

touched a man in years and here she was playing
with fire. The most potentially dangerous fire she'd
ever dealt with: the man had the power to take
away the one person she loved most in this world,
the only family she had left. Alex was smooth and
cultured and used to getting his way no matter
what. Could she have picked anyone worse to...?

To what?

What exactly were they doing?

Well, it didn't matter because it wouldn't happen
again.

Chapter Nine

Alex hadn't intended to kiss Julianne. It was the last thing he should've done. He'd let things slip completely out of control. Yet, it had nearly turned him inside out to feel her surrender in his arms. To give up control—even if it was only for a few minutes.

Still, it was a mistake—especially when his son was sleeping in the next room and the word *lawyer* had been fresh on Julianne's tongue.

It was odd that the nasty word hadn't left a bad aftertaste. No, she'd tasted just as sweet and sexy as he'd imagined. In fact, the kiss had left him craving more. The next time, it could come back to bite him. The one way to ensure it wouldn't was to make sure there wasn't a next time.

Their relationship was already precarious, and Julianne was in his life long-term because she was Liam's aunt. She wasn't like the other women, the ones he could *kiss and dismiss*. She was there whether he liked it or not. He couldn't muddy the waters.

He knocked on her door a couple of minutes early because he wanted to talk to her before they met Luc and Sophie for dinner. He had to set the record straight, to explain that he knew he'd overstepped. That even though he was devastatingly attracted to her, it wouldn't happen again.

His heartbeat kicked up a notch when she opened the door. She was in her bathrobe, barefoot, her hair still a little damp, as if he'd interrupted her blow drying.

Despite her sexy, tousled appearance, the look on her face told him she'd already been thinking along the same lines as he: Another kiss like that wasn't going to happen again. The ice queen was back. Any traces of the hot-blooded woman who'd made him melt in her arms were gone.

"You're early," she said, immediately turning

and walking toward the living room, expecting him to follow.

"I am," he said. "I wanted to talk to you."

Her toenails were painted hot pink, and the startling color caused his gaze to linger on her feet. He'd only ever seen her in black, which made sense because that was her uniform for the orchestra. To glimpse her not quite so put together, in nothing but a plush white robe with this sexy burst of color at her feet was…so different. And quite alluring, he had to admit, despite the icy glare.

She folded her arms across her chest. "Look, I know what you're going to say—"

Liam's cry sounded from the other room.

She held up a hand. "Excuse me." She turned to go to the boy.

"Wait a minute," he said.

How did she know what he was going to say? Maybe it was going to be something positive. How could she know what he was thinking?

She stopped and turned to look at him.

"Why don't you go finish getting dressed and I'll take care of Liam?"

"No, he wants me."

"If you don't hurry, we're going to be late."

He could tell by the look on her face that she didn't want to give in, but she did.

"Okay, fine. I'll only be a minute. If you could just bring him out here, I have some milk warming in the bottle warmer on the table. Go ahead and give him that and I'll be right out."

He followed the crying into one of the bedrooms and saw Liam standing in the crib, holding on to the rails, his tears subsided to a whimper.

"Hi, little guy," he said. "Your mom…*er*…that is…your aunt…Aunt Julianne is getting ready. You're going to spend some time with your father for little bit. Then we're going to a party. Are you good with that?"

His mom? That was a Freudian slip. Purely accidental.

The boy had stopped crying and was looking at Alex as if trying to understand what he was babbling on about, and perhaps why he wasn't Julianne. Liam looked cute in miniature blue jeans and a tiny shirt with a baseball bat with the word *Slugger* on the front of it. The All-American baby. He wondered if Julianne had dressed him this way on purpose. To send a message?

When Alex held out his arms to Liam, he was surprised the boy let go of the crib with one hand and reached for him.

"Your Papa might not be so bad after all, *oui?*"

He grabbed Liam under his arms and the toddler

squirmed. Alex took a moment to try and figure out the best way to hold the wiggling baby, and Alex finally found a way to awkwardly fit him against his own left shoulder, with his arm firmly under the boy's bottom.

"Are you hungry? I hear there's a bottle out here with your name on it. Let's get you something to eat."

Julianne could hold her own when it came to things like playing music in front of large crowds or fighting for the people she loved, but she was stricken utterly defenseless by the sight of Alex sitting on the couch holding Liam in his arms giving the boy his bottle.

With one little hand, Liam reached up and touched Alex's face. The way father and son gazed at each other was enough to knock the life breath out of her.

No matter how she tried to stop it, the truth seeped in through the cracks in all her reasons why Alex Lejardin had no right to Liam. This picture of father and son, this snapshot of the most unconditional kind of love warmed her and petrified her at the same time.

How could she take Liam's father away from him? But how could she give up her little boy? She loved him, and she'd promised her sister, who'd chosen not to leave him with his father for reasons unknown. Perhaps she needed to get to the bottom of those reasons so she could better understand?

From this vantage point, it seemed like a no-win situation.

If she stayed in Europe for Liam to be near Alex, she'd have to give up her World of Music students and the new opportunity with the reorganized orchestra. Maybe she could get a job here…or in Paris. But principal flutist positions were few and far between. Plus, she didn't have the money to move nor the visa that would allow her to work. Sure, between Alex and her they could probably somehow make it work, but at what cost? And through how many miles of red tape?

On the flip side, if she went back to Washington, she'd have to give up Liam because…well, this picture in front of her of this big, strong man holding this little boy…the love emanating from his eyes…that was the reason.

Alex obviously loved his son—although she didn't want to admit it, probably as much as she loved Liam in his own way. She'd have to be pretty heartless to want to separate them. But could she just turn over this little boy to a man who received death threats? It wouldn't be like *this* every day.

Alex would go back to work in his Parisian office. Who would watch Liam? Would he be raised by a stranger who stood in for the majority of Liam's life, except for the brief time when Alex's job allowed him to pop in?

Alex looked up and smiled when he realized she was standing there.

"Not bad for a guy who's never given a baby a bottle, don't you think?"

Nope, not bad at all.

"You're a fast learner."

Suddenly, she remembered the clean, grassy masculine scent of him as she'd been in his arms, and the way he'd looked when he'd leaned in and kissed her. She willed away the image.

He'd come early to talk to her, and she knew he was the kind of man who was going to lay his cards on the table about their involvement. Their kiss. Their whatever. But after holding and feeding Liam, there was a completely different vibe about Alex. She hoped he wouldn't bring up the kiss. Not only did she not want to talk about it, but she also didn't want his excuses or explanations. She just wanted to get this night over with. Maybe tomorrow, after a good night's sleep—if that was possible—she'd get a clear-cut sense about what to do.

Because right now, standing here watching Alex with Liam, there was no doubt they were family. Just where she fit in was unclear. She felt more alone than she had since she'd lost Marissa.

Even though they didn't have to leave the castle, it seemed like they had to walk a good half mile to get to Sophie and Luc's apartment.

They'd taken the elevator up three floors where a petite redhead named Patrice, the royal family's social secretary, met them.

"Good evening," she said. "Please follow me and I'll let Queen Sophie and His Highness know you're here."

The walls of the marble hallway had a similar museum feel to the floor where they were staying, more grand. It was a little unnerving. But the reception they received when they walked in was much more down-to-earth.

Julianne didn't know whether to curtsey or bow or…but before she could figure it out, Sophie had hugged her and plucked Liam out of her arms and was cooing and bouncing him.

The queen was a willowy, gorgeous, green-eyed brunette who sported a little baby bump front and center. Julianne liked her instantly because she got a sense that Sophie was her own woman. Being a commoner for so many years before assuming the throne probably made Sophie more grounded than the average thirty-something queen. Still, she possessed a quiet, commanding grace.

If Liam grew up here, did it mean he'd benefit from the same down-to-earth upbringing? While living in a castle? With his own staff of Secret Service agents trailing him everywhere he went? *Right.*

She met Luc, Sophie's handsome husband, and Henri, the middle brother, who was the state minister of arts and culture.

What a good-looking trio of men, Julianne marveled, as she watched Alex greet his brothers with handshakes that morphed into slap-on-the-back man-hugs.

"What a precious little boy," Sophie said as she planted a kiss on Liam's cheek. "We don't know what we're going to have." She placed a hand on her stomach. "We already have a daughter, Savannah. So a boy would be nice, but really I don't care just as long as the baby is healthy."

"Speaking of Savannah," Alex said, "where is she?"

"She's off on a class trip to Italy," said Sophie. She turned to Julianne. "Savannah is actually my daughter from a previous marriage. She's sixteen, and she's Alex's biggest fan. When we first arrived in St. Michel, she had such a crush on Alex."

So he does have that effect on all women, Julianne thought as Alex waved away Sophie's teasing.

"She's a great kid, very sweet and endearing," Alex added. "Going on a class trip without parents in tow? That has to be a teenager's dream. If the princess leads such a full life, maybe Liam won't have such a bad time here after all."

He and Julianne locked gazes. Julianne kept her face neutral. He'd said that for her benefit, of course. Or to bait her. But she wasn't biting. If she opened for debate the topic of Liam living in St. Michel, she'd be too outnumbered. Alex had nearly all of his family here—each one was taking turns holding and fussing over the baby. She refused to put Liam at the center of such a terribly lopsided tug-of-war.

How long would she be able to stave them off?

Sophie linked her arm through Julianne's and escorted her over to the sofa. "How about some champagne?"

"Yes, please," Julianne said. "I'd love some."

As if by magic, a server with a tray of filled glasses appeared. Until that moment Julianne hadn't noticed him. She accepted the champagne and then a piece of pâté on toast offered to her from a tray presented by another server.

"Julianne, I understand that you are a musician," Henri said.

"Yes, I am a flutist." She started to add, with the Continental Symphony Orchestra, but bit off the words before they escaped. She didn't feel like explaining that the orchestra had folded. It sounded so tragic. Actually, it was tragic—and it was too early to announce anything about a possible reorganization. Everything, it seemed, was in limbo right now.

"I wish I could've caught their final concert in Paris last week," Henri said. "It's a shame that so many quality orchestras are disbanding."

He knew.

Of course he knew. Music, art and culture were his calling. She tried to convince herself that that was the reason he knew—not because St. Michel's Big Brother had filled him in on it, along with every other detail of her life.

Even though his tone wasn't rude or snide, or otherwise condescending, she felt a little sick, thinking about the possibility that her life was an open book. Ever since she'd introduced Alex to Liam—

Liam? Where was Liam?

Her gaze darted around the room searching for him. Her heart raced until she found him sitting on Sophie's lap in a chair next to the sofa. In the span of thirty seconds of conversation, she'd lost sight of him.

Her knees felt a little weak in the post-adrenaline letdown. He was safe. Not that he wouldn't be. Not that they'd try to distract her with a party while they made off with her baby, but it just—that had never happened before. She'd never carelessly *lost sight* of him. Not when he was with her, which was ninety percent of the time. When Liam was in her care, she was always fully cognizant of where he was.

The scariest part was that it had happened so fast. Well, it would never happen again.

Never.

"Yes, it is a shame, isn't it?" She kept her voice steady as she kept Liam in her peripheral vision.

"Are you currently seeking a position with an orchestra?" Henri asked.

"Yes, I am. I have several irons in the fire right now. I'm waiting to hear back."

"*Bon.* In the meantime, I'd be pleased to introduce you to Maestro Fernand Leroy, the conductor of the St. Michel National Symphony. I'm not sure of the orchestra's needs at the moment. But if the maestro is not auditioning flutists, the orchestra still employs substitutes on occasion. It would be a good contact for you."

Soon the chef called the five of them to dinner. There was a high chair set up for Liam where he enjoyed mashing his freshly mashed vegetables further, while the adults enjoyed a surf-and-turf platter of Kobe beef and lobster tail.

Alex's family kept her so engaged in conversation that there wasn't a chance for things to get awkward—with them or Alex. She was touched that they were making such an effort.

By the time they adjourned to the living room to enjoy a selection of coffee, tea, brandy and chocolates, Julianne had forgotten why she'd been so nervous about meeting them. She took a seat on the couch near the chair where Sophie sat and hugged Liam in her lap. Actually, she hadn't completely forgotten why she'd been worried—and, of course, all the challenges ahead of them hadn't been solved by one civil dinner. Really, the subject hadn't even been broached, much less sorted out. But at first glance, this royal family, with their power and money, seemed to be playing fair.

As Julianne sipped a cup of lavender chamomile tea, she tried to resist the scrumptious-looking assortment of chocolates arranged on the silver tray that graced the center of the coffee table. Caffeine right before bed—especially in the form of chocolate—was a recipe for a night of tossing and turning. Even with the soothing tea.

Resistance was futile after all, and Julianne plucked a dark-chocolate-powder-dusted truffle off the tray.

She bit into it and it melted like a silky river of heaven on her tongue.

"Ummm," she couldn't help herself. "This is *so*…decadent. I think it's the best chocolate I've ever tasted. What kind is it?"

Sophie smiled and claimed a piece for herself. "I know, isn't it delicious? Believe it or not, it's made right here in St. Michel. It's from Maya's Chocolate Shop, downtown off the square. It's my favorite dessert."

Julianne was dying to ask if this was how she and Luc lived every day—and if so, how she stayed so trim. She carried her baby bump front and center, and there wasn't an excess ounce on her willowy figure. Or was the special treatment and delicious food strictly reserved for guests? Or, more specifically, guests they wanted to placate?

As warm and gracious as Sophie and Luc

had been tonight, Julianne felt bad for being so cynical.

"Alex tells me you've started a music foundation?" Sophie asked.

Julianne nodded.

"Please tell me about it."

Julianne gave Sophie the pitch. "Currently, we serve about a hundred kids between the ages of ten and seventeen in the Washington, D.C., area, providing music lessons and instruments to those who need them. Our services supplement their school music program. We're hoping to gain more support soon so that we can reach even more kids."

Sophie listened intently. "That's tremendous. I understand that your focus has been in your hometown, but perhaps you could work with our national orchestra's music outreach program, and give them some pointers on setting up a similar program here? If you would, we might be inclined to support you in the expansion of your D.C.-based venture."

The thought made Julianne's head spin. She hadn't thought about taking her program international. But why not? After all, the program was called A World of Music. Wouldn't it be magnificent to bring music into the lives of every child in the world?

"That sounds very exciting. I'd be happy to help."

Sophie smiled at her warmly. "Just so you know, we can provide you with a babysitter any time you need one. Especially to help with your foundation work, but for personal needs, too. Moms need to take care of themselves. It makes us better moms, doesn't it?"

At first, Julianne thought she'd heard Sophie wrong, *Moms need to take care of themselves,* but when she'd said it the second time, she knew it was true.

Julianne bit her bottom lip to keep from smiling too big. Then she realized she'd missed what Sophie was saying…something about moving office equipment into her suite so that she could more efficiently run the foundation…

Wow. It was so much, so fast. "I am grateful, really I am. The only problem is that the administrative end of A World of Music needs minimal upkeep. Most of it is hands-on—delivering instruments, and teaching lessons." Julianne cleared her throat delicately before speaking, stalling for just the right words—she didn't want to sound ungrateful. "While I'm here, my kids are missing their flute lessons."

"I suppose you'll need to find someone else to

take over the lessons for you," said Luc. "The rest you can run from here."

Wait a minute. Julianne's gratitude began to backpedal into something a little more cautious.

"I don't know if that will be necessary since I don't know how long Liam and I will be staying."

A hush fell over the room, as if Julianne had just pulled a skeleton out of a closet and dropped it in front of them.

"Of course, we'll come as often as we can for visits, but our home is in Washington, D.C. It's what my sister, Marissa, wanted for Liam."

As her sister's name rolled off her tongue, she realized it was the first time that evening anyone had even mentioned Marissa. For a split second Julianne wondered if anyone even knew about her... knew the full story.

Surely they did because their intelligence agents seemed to be able to dig up everything about everybody once it was on their radar.

Alex was looking at her solemnly. "We obviously have a lot to iron out."

His voice sounded apologetic.

But then Liam started to fuss and it was the perfect time to excuse herself. After the day's travel she was tired.

"Thank you so much for everything, dinner was delicious," Julianne said. "If you don't mind, I think I need to get Liam settled for the evening. He's had a long, hard day."

Sophie smiled warmly. "Of course, you must be exhausted, too. It's so nice to meet you. I'm very glad you're here. We'll have to set up a girls' lunch, just the two of us. Perhaps later this week? We can discuss the music foundation."

"That would be nice." Julianne stood with Liam on her hip, feeling a little less at ease as she had earlier. Of course, the reason for the dinner hadn't been simply to welcome her. It had been to size her up, to see if she'd slide easily into the slot they had picked out for her.

It was surprising that they hadn't just informed her that along with her new country and her new apartment, they had already decided to assign her to their orchestra…. Enough. She was tired and it had been a nice evening. She didn't want to dampen it any more than she already had.

She tried to push the straps of Liam's diaper bag upon one of her shoulders, but the large purse slid back down to her elbow with a jolting thud.

Alex was at her side to help.

"Let me carry that," Alex insisted. "I'll walk you back to your suite."

His hand was on her arm. Somehow, he'd managed to slip his fingers beneath the strap and her arm, relieving the pressure where it cut into the crook of her elbow. The warmth of his hand spread over the sensitive skin there, reminding her of how his hands had felt on her body earlier that day when he'd kissed her. Her pulse quickened and she was sure he could feel it. If not, the heat creeping up her neck must've been a dead giveaway that his touch made her anxious.

"You're not ready to leave yet, are you?" she asked. "Really, please stay and talk to your brothers. I'm sure you have a lot of catching up to do."

"Yes, we would like a little more time with him," Luc told Julianne. "That is, if you truly don't mind."

A rush of relief washed over Julianne. She'd rather not have the long walk back to their twin suites, nor the awkward pause and stilted goodnights at the door. Not after their kiss today. Not after the simple touch of his hand taking the diaper bag from her caused her to flush like one of the vestal virgins caught in an act of impropriety.

"I don't mind at all. In fact, I insist."

"Thank you, Julianne," Luc said. "I'll call someone to escort you back."

* * *

After Julianne left with her escort, Sophie excused herself, leaving the three brothers alone to talk.

Luc refilled their brandy snifters while Henri got up and stoked the logs in the giant fireplace.

Alex swirled the liquid in his glass and contemplated the warm amber color, fighting the feeling that he should've insisted on walking Julianne and Liam back to the room.

But the truth was he needed to put some distance between them. He needed to not lead her on, and walking her home as if they'd been on a date might mislead her into drawing that conclusion. Although, if circumstances were different—if Liam weren't in the middle—he would want to date her.

It was the truth.

But in this case, truth and necessity were enemies.

"So, our little brother is a father." Henri chuckled. "Looks like it's time to finally pay the fiddler."

Alex didn't see the humor in this. "While we're tossing around clichés, isn't that like the pot calling the kettle black?"

Henri held up his hands. "I don't have any little ones running around. I'm careful about that."

Alex frowned. "Yeah, well, so was I."

Or at least he'd thought he was until that night. The night that should never have happened.

"Did you have a paternity test?" Luc asked.

Alex's heart gave a weird twisting sensation as Liam's face appeared in his mind's eye.

"He's mine," Alex said. "All you have to do is look at him to see that."

If the night hadn't happened, then he wouldn't have Liam. It was the strangest, most inexplicable dichotomy. He loved the boy, even if he'd never been in love with the boy's birth mother. A birth mother who was no longer alive and had given his child to her sister, to whom Alex was attracted.

But because of Marissa, the attraction should be a moot point; because of Liam, Julianne would forever be in his life, presenting one of those unfortunate you-can-read-the-menu-but-you-can't-eat situations.

Unfortunately, every time he looked at Julianne he was ravenous.

"This is the first woman you've ever brought home to meet the family."

Luc's voice startled him back to the present. Alex sipped his brandy to buy time.

"I didn't bring her home. I brought my son home."

"Technically, you did bring her home," Henri interjected. "Even if you wanted to bring your child here, you didn't have to bring his aunt to St. Michel."

Alex acknowledged the truth in what his brother said with a shrug. "They're a package deal. That's actually a huge problem."

The room smelled lightly of smoke and the fine leather furniture and the long-stemmed white roses displayed in vases around the room.

Roses were among the notes in Julianne's perfume. The thought floated absently through his head, settling in the back of his mind, along with the way she tasted and the ragged, sexy sound of her breathing as they'd come up for air after the kiss.

He wanted to taste her again.

"How is that a problem?" asked Luc.

"Pourquoi?" Henri chimed in. "She's gorgeous, smart, seems very attached to Liam."

"It's more complicated than I can explain."

"We have all night," Henri said.

Alex knew now was as good a time as any to confide in his brothers about the circumstances surrounding Marissa, Liam and Julianne.

"How old are you now?" Luc asked.

Thirty.

"Old enough to know better," Alex said.

Luc grimaced. "Exactly. Everything changes when there's a child involved. You've had a chance to live, when are you going to settle down?"

Alex bristled at the question, staring silently into his snifter.

"It sounds like I'm lecturing you. I'm not. Of course, I'm not. Liam is welcome to stay here, but a child should not be raised by nannies when he has two loving parents. Of course, nannies help, but they shouldn't take the place of a parent. How are you and Julianne going to work this out?"

"I have no idea. Liam's safety is what I'm concerned about right now. The threats I've received from a rather militant group of terrorists are serious. And, as we've discussed, they apply to the rest of the family and close friends."

"So, by virtue of Liam, Julianne could be in danger, too?"

Alex nodded. "I'm sorry she had to be dragged into this. I'm sorry Liam had to be born into this. But these types of threats are the reason I'd decided I was never getting married and having a family. I knew it was a choice when I chose this career path. After what happened to mom…" Alex's voice cracked.

As St. Michel's former minister of security, Luc had been their father's successor in the position. Luc knew better than anyone the toll that a job in law enforcement could take—he'd given it up once he'd fallen in love with Sophie. Then again, the extenuating circumstances of her being the heir to the throne had been a contributing factor, but the bottom line was that Luc had chosen love over the adrenaline rush of law and order.

Even though Alex had initially chosen a career in law—and Henri had shunned the family tradition altogether—Alex had ended up following in their father's footsteps after all, when he took the position at iWITNESS.

That's also when he'd decided he'd never marry and have a family. It was too hard to do both. It wasn't fair for the loved ones waiting at home.

Loved ones who often turned into sitting ducks and pawns for schemes of retribution.

Alex and his brothers were intimately acquainted with the terror and sorrow; their mother had paid the ultimate price.

Her life had been taken as retribution for their father's putting away a terrorist who'd made an attempt on the late King Bertrand's life.

After losing their mother, the boys—their family—had never been quite the same. It was the catalyst that drove Alex away from St. Michel, away from thoughts of family and death. It had only been since they were older that the brothers had come back together as friends.

Alex cleared his throat. "I'm just saying, it's not fair to put anyone through that kind of life."

"I don't know," said Luc. "Since the boy regards Julianne as a mother figure, and it's obvious he does, she will always be a part of your life."

"That's a given." Alex swirled the brandy in his snifter and nodded.

"Her home is in Washington," he continued. "How are you going to make this work? Are you going to share custody?"

Alex's head jerked up at the suggestion. "I'm not sending Liam to Washington. It won't work. It's not safe, and I don't want him that far away. Plus, shipping a baby back and forth on long overseas flights wouldn't be the best thing for him."

The fire crackled.

Henri, who'd been uncharacteristically quiet finally contributed. "Well, then, it sounds like the best thing for everyone is to convince Julianne to move here or to Paris."

Alex shook his head. "Easier said than done.

Even if I could convince her to pack up and leave her life back in Washington to start over in Paris, which is where I'll be, where I want Liam to be, there would be the issue of visas."

"Unless you get married," Luc said.

Alex quashed every positive emotion that the thought dredged up, Marriage—to anyone—was not for him. Not even for his son's sake. And certainly not when it involved a woman for whom he was starting to develop deep feelings.

Chapter Ten

Downtown St. Michel was a gorgeous little medieval storybook village. Storefronts with hand-painted signs lined a cobblestone square, with narrow streets jutting into it like spokes of a wheel. They passed a butcher and a baker...and Julianne was sure they'd stumble upon a candlestick maker before the day was through.

Turning her face into the sunshine, she was glad she let Alex convince her to get out today.

She'd awakened to find a voice message from him: *"Are we still on for sailing today and/or a tour of St. Michel? Please call or text once you're up and around."*

Julianne had been reluctant to spend the day with Alex, feeling as awkward as she was after telling his family she and Liam wouldn't be staying in St. Michel. Now that she was rested and they were outside with Liam in a stroller enjoying the fresh morning air, things were starting to feel better.

"There's a great little patisserie around the corner," Alex said. "Why don't we get some pastry and take it with us on the boat?"

It was chilly out, but not as cold as it had been in Paris. In fact, if they stayed out of the shadows of the buildings and walked in the sun, it was quite pleasant. "I could use a strong cup of coffee to go with that good pastry."

Alex smiled at her. "Follow me."

He was looking particularly good this morning in jeans and a moss-colored polo shirt that brought out the green in his eyes. As he picked up the pace, walking a few steps ahead, she noticed that his gorgeous eyes weren't his only asset.

Yeah. She'd definitely spent worse days with far less attractive people.

The downtown square was free of people except for a couple of merchants sweeping their entryways and an artist painting at his easel. Liam seemed to be happy to be outside in the fresh air. He was sitting up in his stroller, taking in everything. He pointed to a cat perched on a windowsill, only to be distracted by a black dog lolling in the doorway of the cheese shop.

She remembered what Alex had said about March being off season, and was grateful for this insider's look at the town.

Julianne drew in a deep breath and was treated to the tantalizing aroma of fresh baking bread mingling with a hint of cinnamon, vanilla and... chocolate. The scent was so tempting that it made her mouth water.

The chocolate shop that Sophie had mentioned at dinner last night had to be close by.

"Are you familiar with Maya's Chocolate Shop?" Julianne asked.

"It's a legend," Alex said.

"I'd really like to visit it before we leave today." She inhaled another whiff of the chocolate which was calling to her, and when she glanced at Alex, she noticed he was looking at her in a particular way that made her feel as if she'd intruded on something private. Awkwardly, she cleared her throat.

"I can smell the chocolate. It has to be close by."

He picked up his pace and walked slightly ahead of her once more. They turned a tight corner that led them to a street that was more of an ancient alleyway than a road built for anything other than pedestrian traffic.

"There you go," Alex said, pointing upward toward a sign.

Julianne followed the direction of his finger to a hand-painted sign that read *Maya's Chocolate Shop.*

The shop window was adorned with white lace curtains and was brimming with tins and boxes tied with colorful ribbon. Pyramids of chocolate were arranged on several glass-dome covered stands; even more—chocolate-dipped fruit, bon-bons, truffles, petits fours—were set out in bounti-ful exhibits on doily-covered trays.

It was a feast for the eyes that tempted Julianne to press her nose against the glass.

Maybe it was the allure of decadence, or perhaps just the promise of what she'd tasted last night, but Julianne was drawn to the shop like the eye would be pulled to a shiny coin caught between the cobblestones.

"Alex, I want to go in," she said, nearly breathless.

"Of course," he said. "Why don't you go in there and I'll get the coffee and pastries? Unless you want to see the patisserie?"

He seemed eager to get to the boat. Of course, the downtown area was probably old hat to him, good for nothing more than a bakery indulgence.

"Go ahead," Julianne said.

"I'll meet you and Liam back here."

Before he left, he pulled opened the glass shop door for her. A wind chime sounded, and Julianne was immediately struck by the scrumptious scent of chocolate as she'd never smelled it before. Alex held the door open until she'd maneuvered the stroller inside.

"I'll see you in a minute," he said. As he closed the door, the chimes sounded again.

"Bonjour!" a lilting voice rang out.

"Bonjour," Julianne answered, suddenly wishing she'd asked Alex to stay to serve as interpreter. She'd not brought her lexicon and had forgotten that French was the St. Michelian native language. Sophie was so *American*. Maybe that's why she and Julianne had related so well.

At first, Julianne didn't see where the voice had come from. She glanced around the shop, taking in the copper candy molds decorating one wall, the gift baskets artfully arranged on glass shelving, the confectionery displays adorning the case, and the marble wrap table standing regally in the center of it all. That's when she caught a glimpse of curly, fire-red hair and a woman whose expression was nearly as vibrant.

"Hello," said the woman, as she stepped out from behind a display. This time she greeted her in heavily accented English. "Good morning."

The woman's broad smile was nearly as warm as the color of her hair. "Well, look at you," she said. "There's a woman in love if I've ever seen one."

For the span of a heartbeat, Julianne was too shocked by the woman's suggestion to move. She glanced behind herself to make sure Alex wasn't still standing there, even though she knew he'd gone and would've heard the chimes if he'd come back into the shop.

"The only person I'm in love with is this little guy right here," Julianne said, finally recovering her good sense.

The redhead tilted her head to the side and furrowed her brow as if something didn't make sense.

Finally, she shrugged.

"Well, if not now, soon. Very soon." She nodded resolutely. "Don't worry, everything will work out fine."

If not now, soon. Very soon.

Julianne blushed as she replayed the words in

her head. The woman had audacity to assume such things.

What? Did she fancy herself some sort of psychic?

"I'm Maya. What may I get for you?"

Despite her bold comments, warmth seemed to radiate out of Maya's every pore. Julianne felt every bit as drawn to her as she did the tiny little shop.

After Alex had steered them safely out of the harbor, he set the sailboat's steering lock and turned his attention to the chocolates Julianne offered him. He pulled the ribbon from the small white box. Inside were two heart-shaped pieces of dark chocolate.

"Did you pick these out?" he asked.

"No, Maya gave them to me, one for each of us. Why?"

An odd sense of letdown tempered his mood.

She looked gorgeous sitting there in her turtleneck sweater and windbreaker, hugging Liam in his little orange life vest, trying to keep the boy wrapped in a blanket to shield him from the wind.

It was warmer today, and Liam didn't seem to be at all bothered by the wind or the sea spray. In fact, Liam kept alternately sticking his head up so that the spray misted his face and then burying his head against Julianne's chest, in a game of sorts.

Alex loved watching them, the way they interacted, the way the wind whipped Julianne's dark hair, the way her eyes rivaled the color of the Côte d'Azur.

He took his piece of candy and handed her the box.

She peered into the box, to see what it held while keeping it far enough away that Liam couldn't grab it.

"Oh." Her gaze flicked from the contents of the box to meet his eyes. Color flooded her cheeks.

Why was she blushing?

Maybe for the same reason he'd thought a piece of heart-shaped chocolate might have had some significance. What was wrong with him? In the past, if he'd thought for a moment that a woman was giving him chocolate hearts, that would've been the precise moment he would have turned his boat around and politely sent her back to shore.

Then again, when was the last time he'd taken a woman out on his boat?

"Maya is a piece of work," she said. "Do you know her?"

"No. Before today, I'd never had the pleasure."

Julianne had introduced him when he'd gotten

back to the shop after fetching their pastries. Then it had only been a quick *bonjour* and they'd said goodbye, ready to head to the boat. In fact, he hadn't realized the chocolates had been a gift, or there would've been a *merci* with the *bonjour*.

"She claims her chocolates have medicinal properties," Julianne said. "That the right piece of chocolate can help a person solve their problems."

"Sounds to me like she's a great business-woman," Alex murmured before biting into his piece of candy.

"Mmm…" The throaty note of pleasure escaped before he knew what he was doing. He glanced at Julianne just as she bit into hers. Although she was a little less vocal, a bit more delicate about her pleasure, bliss was definitely written all over her pretty features.

"I think I might need a daily dose of this medicine," he murmured. He didn't realize he'd said it aloud until Julianne answered him.

"Oh, do you have a sweet tooth?"

He hadn't been talking about the chocolate.

"Yes, something like that. What's in the chocolate?" He peered at the bit of candy that remained. It contained flecks of red.

"I think those are rose petals," Julianne said. "Whatever they are, they're delicious."

As Alex unlocked the wheel and steered the boat, he watched the rapturous look on Julianne's face as she savored the last bite of chocolate. Luc's suggestion that he marry her elbowed its way to the forefront of his mind. Last night, the thought had terrified him. Today, it still didn't sit well, but at least it didn't give him the urge to jump overboard and swim toward shore.

No, today his thoughts were tiptoeing around the fact that marriage was nothing to be taken lightly. Especially when one had a job as dangerous as his with iWITNESS. It was one thing to put himself in harm's way, but it was quite another to drag a woman and child into it.

His heart clenched as he inwardly acknowledged how Liam, by virtue of being his son, had been dragged into it without asking. That's why Alex would make the boy's safety his top priority.

Reflexively, he glanced over his shoulder to the motorboat that was trailing about one hundred yards behind him, with secret service agents on board no doubt surveying the area with high-powered binoculars, ready to move at a moment's notice.

That's the kind of life he lived.

There was no need to drag a woman like Julianne into it. Even if he did like the way she looked, the way she thought…and the way she tasted. Especially since he was still fighting an uncomfortable feeling that he could be quite comfortable with this woman.

For her own good, he couldn't fall in love with her.

As he popped the last bite of the chocolate heart into his mouth, he decided it was a good time to change the subject. "So, how was your time in Paris?"

"Very short," she said.

He'd loved going to her concert and regretted that the evening had ended on such a bad note. He watched her now as she tipped her face into the ocean spray in a new mimicking game with Liam.

"Did you get to see the sights you wanted to see?"

"Basically, all I saw of Paris was the route from the airport to the hotel, then from the hotel to your office, in an hour at Luxembourg Gardens and the Boulevard St. Michel and less than that in the area around the Opéra Garnier."

She held up one free palm in *ta-da* fashion to punctuate the sentence.

"No Eiffel Tower?"

"No."

"No Arc de Triomphe or Champs-Elysées or Louvre?"

"Um, no."

"You're telling me that on your first visit to Paris you basically saw nothing?"

"That about sums it up. I spent the majority of my free time talking to you about Liam. Oh, but I did manage to take a lovely unexpected side trip to St. Michel. The principality. Not the boulevard. Or—er—in addition to the short walk down the Parisian boulevard."

The look she shot him was anything but appreciative.

"I'm sorry," he shot back. "I hope you'll let me make it up to you."

She rolled her eyes. "Right. When would that happen?"

"Actually, I have some business in Paris next week. Why don't you come with me?"

She squinted at him as if he'd suggested they fly back to Paris via the power of flapping their arms.

"I'm serious."

Her expression softened, she looked a little vulnerable, hugging Liam close, as if she were actually considering it.

At that moment, he realized he hoped she was.

"I think Liam has had enough back-and-forth travel for a while."

She bit off the sentence as if she'd considered saying more, but stopped. He hoped she wasn't thinking about letting Liam rest up for the long journey back to the States.

He didn't have the energy to keep fighting that battle. Soon enough they'd have to iron things out—

Marry her. Luc's voice whispered in the back of Alex's mind. He ignored it and tried to return to his original thought of how they'd eventually work out something.

But right now, with the rich taste of chocolate in his mouth and the sweet sight of Julianne holding his baby, all he wanted to think about was…right now.

Or getting her back to Paris.

"We could leave Liam at the palace," he said. "I know Sophie would insist on him staying with her. Sophie would have an entire staff of nannies and her daughter Savannah there to look after him."

Julianne paled at the suggestion and shot him another slightly angry are-you-out-of-your-mind? look.

"I'm completely serious," he responded as if she'd said the words out loud. "I think it would be good for both of us to get away, to put things into perspective. He'd be safer at the palace than—"

"I know," Julianne cut him off. "You keep saying that. But it wouldn't matter if the castle had a moat and drawbridge, I'm not leaving him. And while we're on the subject, I think you should know that this is one of the biggest problems I have about the thought of leaving Liam in St. Michel—not that I've seriously considered it or ever will…for the record. You don't think twice about leaving him behind when he's an inconvenience. That's exactly the kind of thing that Marissa said you would do."

Hearing her name had the same effect as if a wave had splashed up over the side of the boat and doused him.

"Marissa said that to you?"

Julianne looked a little sheepish. "In so many words. Alex, I told you that in her will, her adoption instructions for Liam specifically stated that I was to have custody of Liam because you're irresponsible."

Now, Julianne was making him mad.

"And I told you that she had no idea how I'd be with Liam because she never told me about him."

Hearing his name, Liam whipped his head

around and stared wide-eyed at Alex. Alex wanted to kick himself for using such an abrupt tone and purposely softened his next words.

"It's not irresponsible to have some time to yourself, Julianne. Since Liam has been in your life, how many nights have you spent away from him?"

"None." She said the word as if she deserved accolades.

"That's not healthy," he quipped, tightening the sail lines.

"No, it's not healthy for Liam to be stuck away while you live footloose and fancy-free as if you hadn't a care in the world."

"Footloose and fancy-free? What the—" His gaze slid to Liam as he stifled the oath. "What does that mean?"

She shook her head and gazed out at the horizon as if she wouldn't dignify his question with an answer.

"If you're insinuating that I'm taking the easy way out, you're wrong."

She still wouldn't look at him.

"Now that he's in my life it's not easy for me to contemplate leaving his side for a single minute. But I know that's not healthy for either of us. Julianne, look at me."

She didn't.

"Look at me," he repeated. "I know from experience what it's like to lose someone you love. I understand that. I suspect that living with loss is something we have in common. We know it doesn't just happen to other people, right?"

Now, he'd gotten her attention, but her face was defiant.

"When I was ten, my mother was killed. My father, who was St. Michel's security minister, helped prosecute the head of a crime family and out of retribution…to get the last word, that family murdered my mother. In cold blood. She'd never done a damn thing to anyone and—" His voice broke on the last word and now it was his turn to look away from her.

She gave him a moment, and when he looked back at her, she said, "I'm sorry." True sadness clouded her eyes.

"That's why I never wanted a family, but I have a son and I'll go to any length to protect him. Do you know how easy it would be to smother him with protection? To get so crazy that he doesn't have a normal life? That's why I'm forcing myself to leave him here and go to Paris. He'll be safe here and I'll be a better parent when I return in a few days. Fear of loss. You and I have that in common."

She looked at him with huge, haunted blue eyes and whispered, "Why didn't you tell me this before, Alex? I had no idea. I am so sorry you had to go through that."

He nodded his sad gratitude.

"I've never talked about that with anyone other than my brothers."

Later, that night, as Alex lay in his bed, sleep escaped him despite the day spent sailing. Exercise in the open air was apparently no match for an unfinished conversation with Julianne. They hadn't revisited his suggestion that she accompany him when he returned to Paris.

But he didn't intend to go alone. They needed that time together. For what—other than putting an end to their stalemate over where Liam would live—he wasn't sure.

Even so, the question kept knocking around in the back of his brain, demanding attention in much the same way that Luc's suggestion kept rearing it's scary head, the idea that this might be as good a time as any for Alex to settle down.

He and Julianne and Liam would make a good family. There was no doubt about that. She and the baby were already in the middle of his messy life. There was no extracting them from that. Even if Julianne decided to go back to the States alone, he'd still send security to watch over her, until he was satisfied she was safe.

That she wouldn't meet a similar ugly fate as... he turned over and punched his pillow into shape and replaced the horrible thought with visions of Julianne and Liam...the way they'd looked on the boat today.

There was no denying he was attracted to her. She moved him in a way that Marissa never had.

But even though there was something there with Julianne, he wasn't sure if he could ever love her— what was love anyway? He'd never felt any other kind than the type he had for his brothers...and Liam. A father's love for his son ran even deeper than brotherly love.

It was a different kind of love that was both immediate and unstoppable.

Maybe these feelings that were so hard to comprehend meant there was hope for him after all.

As he lay there plagued by the memory of how Julianne had felt in his arms, Alex grabbed his phone off the bedside table and sent her a text: *Actually the palace does have a moat and drawbridge. For the record.*

Chapter Eleven

"I had a feeling I'd see you today," Maya said to Julianne when she entered the store. "Where's your baby?"

"He's…" She considered her words for a moment. It probably wouldn't do to tell her she was staying at the palace. It would simply be too much to explain.

"He's with friends, at their place."

This solo excursion was an experiment of sorts. Alex was working today and she'd decided to make a quick trip into town. Alone. Or as alone as she could be with the Men in Black following her.

The way Alex had opened up yesterday had

touched her. The way he'd shared with her a personal hurt and torment that no one besides his brothers knew about was moving. And he had a point—to a certain extent—about how being a "hovercraft" parent wasn't healthy for anyone.

Even though she'd been in St. Michel for only three days, after meeting Sophie, Luc and Henri, she knew they weren't going to do anything rash like kidnapping Liam. If they were going to do that, why would they have allowed her to come to St. Michel in the first place?

Still, she'd never left Liam with anyone other than Anita. So this was an exercise as much for her own growth as it was for Liam to get used to being without her—for short periods.

"Bon," said Maya. "Have a seat and we'll have some hot chocolate. I make the best in all of Europe."

Maya gestured to an iron café table situated by the window. Julianne took a seat while Maya went behind the counter and began to brew the chocolate.

"So where is that handsome *amoureux* of yours?"

Julianne's stomach did a flip at the sudden mention of Alex.

"He's not exactly *my amoureux*, as you say."

"But you would like for him to be."

It wasn't a question, it was a bold statement that reached right down into Julianne's insides and gave a little twist.

"Well, no." Julianne answered in a very pathetic way that made her sound like she didn't even know her own mind. Funny how sometimes when she was around Alex, she didn't.

It took a few moments for Maya to brew the chocolate, but by the time she sat down with Julianne to enjoy it they were already deep into conversation.

Twenty-nine-year-old Maya had no qualms about telling Julianne her life story: She was single, but looking; she'd inherited the chocolate shop from her mother because none of her four sisters was interested in the family business. "Perhaps because *Maman* named the shop after her eldest daughter?" Maya suggested with a hint of mischief sparkling in her eyes.

In addition to being the world's best chocolate maker, Maya claimed to have a sixth sense for matchmaking, which made Julianne squirm. Despite how Maya had a way about her that made her feel like an old friend and tempted Julianne to open up, Julianne held firm to talking general terms when it came to Alex and his family—no specifics about Alex's job, other than it involved human rights and that he had family here and that's who they were staying with as they tried to sort out who would have primary custody of Liam.

"You both need to raise the boy," Maya said, in that outspoken, matter-of-fact manner that Julianne had come to realize was her way. "You three are a family, I saw that right away when he opened the door and you stepped into my shop. There was a strong aura of love."

Julianne blew out a breath of dissent. "I don't believe in auras and all that New Agey hogwash."

She glanced at her watch and gasped. "Oh, my gosh, I can't believe how late it is. I have to go."

"Wait, just one moment." Maya jumped up from the table and scurried behind the chocolate cases. "I have something that I think will help you listen to your heart."

Moments later, her new friend emerged with a small white box tied up with a red satin ribbon, identical to the one she'd given Julianne yesterday. Maya slipped it into a bag and handed it to Julianne.

"How much do I owe you?" Julianne asked.

Maya waved away her question.

"You must let me pay you."

"You may pay me by playing your flute in my

shop someday. I think my customers would enjoy that immensely."

It struck Julianne that the entire time she'd been there—both times, in fact—not a single customer had entered the shop.

She adjusted her grip on the bag, feeling guilty for accepting a gift of Maya's chocolate two days in a row—the only two occasions she'd been in her shop.

"I would be thrilled to play in your shop. Think about it and let me know when."

Maya reached out and hugged Julianne. "I will see you soon. After you get back from Paris."

As Julianne walked out the door, a chill washed over her. She hadn't mentioned a thing about going to Paris. She'd talked about having just come *from* Paris, and the possibility of returning home to the States.

But nothing about going to Paris.

Huh… She stopped and looked back at the shop. A gust of wind flirted with the hand-painted sign, making it swing lightly to and fro as if it were waving at her.

Julianne took the box out of the bag and opened it.

Once again, there were two hearts with deep red rose flecks embedded in the dark chocolate.

As she gazed at the two hearts in the box and savored the aroma of deep, rich cocoa, hints of rose and something else a bit more elusive, a portent that everything would be all right washed over her.

"I want you to come to Paris with me," Alex insisted. "I feel guilty that I turned your first trip there into something it shouldn't have been. You should've gone to the top of the Eiffel Tower, not out to the iWITNESS offices. *Mon Dieu,* that place isn't very scenic."

Julianne sat on the couch, gazing down at Liam, giving him a bottle. The boy's eyelids seemed to get heavier and heavier as Liam fought harder to keep his eyes open.

There was a space big enough for another person to occupy between them and Alex.

"Well, gosh, I wonder what I'd be doing right now if I *hadn't* gone out there to see you."

Her voice was low and soothing, a sharp contrast to the take-that look she shot him across the sofa.

He smiled.

"You're funny. You really think you're funny, don't you? I'm asking you to come to Paris with me and you're being snide."

He almost said, *Do you know how many women*

would jump at the chance to go to Paris with me?
But he didn't. Suddenly it didn't seem to matter if
there would ever be another woman in Paris. The
only person he wanted to be there with was her.

She smiled and shrugged, wide-eyed and in-
nocent as if she had no idea what he was talking
about.

He laughed and then bit into the chocolate heart
she'd brought him from Maya's shop. Visions of
what happened the last time the two of them sat
there without the protection of Liam between them
kissed in his mind's eye.

"Okay, I'll go." Her words yanked him back to
the present.

"Okay, great." His mouth was suddenly dry.
"We'll leave tomorrow."

Julianne found Paris's tiled rooftops and wide
boulevards even more beautiful this time. Alex
showed her his favorite spots—both the well-
known spots and off-the-beaten-path haunts.

But her favorite place had to be the top of the
Eiffel Tower.

"This is the best way to get an orientation of
Paris," he said. "You can see everything from up
here."

On one side, he pointed out the Trocadéro. Then

swept her to the other side to point out the Champs de Mars—the green expanse running between the Eiffel Tower and Ecole Militaire and finally, the gold-domed church at Les Invalides.

They spent the rest of the day exploring Montmartre and finally sharing dinner at Alex's favorite restaurant in the sixteenth arrondissement, which Julianne learned simply meant "neighborhood" in French.

It was a glorious day capped off by a heady evening of wine and a moonlit walk back to Alex's apartment, where, along the way, hands brushed and shoulders bumped as they sometimes edged a little too close, blurring the edges between where friends stopped being friends and lovers embarked on that journey of faith. It had been building all day when they finally arrived back at Alex's apartment.

The full moon was shining through the open curtains, and as Julianne stood at the window, Alex came up behind her and put his arms around her as he pointed out the top of the Eiffel Tower in the distance, the place they'd been shining like a promise of what was to come.

Maybe it was the wine, making her feel a little dizzy. But as he kissed her neck and slid his hands under her blouse, the feeling of his skin on hers made her realize with perfect clarity that the only thing she was drunk on was Alex Lejardin.

Even so, bolstered by the liquid courage and so full of want and longing for him, she turned and pressed her palms against his chest, letting her hands linger there, savoring the feel of his firm muscles. Then she slid her hands up and over the expanse of his shoulders, working her way down his arms until her fingers stopped at his wrists behind her.

The movement pressed the most intimate parts of their bodies together, and she could feel his desire.

This was the point of no return. She knew that, as she gazed up at him, searching his face, his eyes, his lips, looking for answers to questions that were becoming increasingly less important by the second. Until finally they were snuffed out altogether as he pulled out of her grasp and enfolded her with his body. He ravished her mouth, bold and hungry—there was nothing tentative between them as there'd been a moment ago or that day in St. Michel when they'd tasted each other for the first time. It was as if every glance, every word, every brush of fingertips today had been leading to this moment.

Without taking his mouth off hers, he backed

her down the hall into a room—his bedroom, she guessed, and tugged her down onto the bed that suddenly appeared underneath her.

He tugged her blouse over her head, then pulled her bra down so that her breasts were naked in the moonlight. When he took a nipple into his mouth, need coursed through her hot and ready.

How long has it been?

She was surprised she didn't melt in his hands. It was the feel of those hands—the touch of his rugged fingers on her smooth skin—that kept her cognizant, though just barely, and made her arch under him, demanding more.

As if they were suspended in time, the world seemed to fade away. Exploring her body with his mouth and hands, he kissed and teased and tormented her, taking her to the brink of places she hadn't visited in a long time.

Her fingers worked his zipper and tugged away his pants until all the barriers between them were gone.

Then he reached into a drawer in the nightstand and pulled out a condom.

As he lowered himself on top of her, her legs parted, greedy for the feel of him, wanting every masculine inch of him to cover her, to weigh her down, to make her body thrum with the pleasure of him. As if reading her mind, he thrust his hips forward and with one bold stroke he entered her.

She gasped from the sheer pleasure of feeling him inside her.

"Are you okay?" he asked.

"Never been better," she whispered, barely able to get the words out.

His breathing rasped against her temple. He pulled out then thrust a little deeper.

Her body clung to him sliding, grabbing, pulsing and releasing over and over until the weight and force of waves of pleasure crashed inside her.

His breath was labored and hot against her cheek until he gave a final thrust and a long, anguished groan erupted in this throat. He collapsed on top of her, kissing her tenderly, possessively as she reveled in their spent pleasure, in the feel of how his broad back narrowed at the waist, at the sheer masculine width and breadth of him. Until he pulled back a little, his lips still brushing hers.

"Marry me," he whispered.

She froze, sure that she'd heard him wrong, but petrified that she hadn't.

"What?" Her hands retreated from his back.

"Marry me," he said again.

She pulled back reclaiming as much personal space as she could and studied him, wondering if he was simply caught up in the moment or if he'd truly lost his mind. Or if he knew how she felt about him, because she was only just beginning to admit those feelings to herself.

He looked a little disoriented, obviously not having had the benefit of the gravity of the shock that had pulled her back down to earth.

"Why?" she asked.

She knew it wasn't romantic to ask *Why?* after having received a marriage proposal, but then again, she had the sickening feeling that this was not a *real* proposal—and if it was, it wasn't for the right reasons.

Alex blinked and propped himself up on his elbow gazing down at her. His eyes searched her face, as if trying to form exactly the right explanation.

"Because..." he started, but his gaze darted away. Julianne watched his expression change until he ended up looking more horrified than like a man in love who was so enraptured he'd proposed. "I think we'd make a good team."

She suddenly felt very exposed lying there and pulled the sheet up to cover herself.

A good team? That was not a reason to get married. A good team. Really?

They were not choosing up sides for kickball.

This was for life, and the only reason you got married was because you loved someone.

Oh, this was wrong on so many levels, and for a moment she was paralyzed by the sobering magnitude of it.

Of course he didn't love her. Even though they'd just made love.

And he had a history with her sister about which he hadn't been very forthcoming.

All that Alex and she had between them was a couple of kisses and one night in Paris that was turning out to be a disaster.

"Julianne, think about it." Now he was lying on his back, with his palm resting on his forehead. "We could make it work. We could be a family— you, Liam and me."

"There are a couple of small problems here," she said.

"What?"

"Number one—We're not in love. And two—My sister still lives between us like a ghost."

He winced. "Your sister was a fine woman, but I never loved her."

"I guess that seems to be a pattern with you, huh? You didn't love her. You don't love me. You've taken us both to bed."

"It's different between you and me."

"How is it different, Alex?" She sat up and hugged her knees to her chest.

"You and Marissa are… I could never see myself with her, but from the first day that you walked into my office, I sensed that we'd…"

"What?"

"That we could work."

She squinted at him for a moment, trying to figure out exactly what he was talking about.

"Think of all the people who get married for *love*," he said, "only to wake up one morning to discover too late that they can't stand each other. At least we *like* each other for who we are. We get along. That's more than I can say for most marriages."

"Really?" she asked. "Are you telling me you don't believe in love?"

"Not in the fairy-tale, happily-ever-after kind that people delude themselves into believing."

She kept herself covered with the sheet as she got up and searched for her clothes. She felt a little sick.

"I thought I knew you, Alex. The *real* you, but obviously, I don't. I've already been in one loveless marriage. I'm not doing it again."

Chapter Twelve

He couldn't have messed that up any worse if he'd tried. Julianne had slept in the guest room and had insisted on leaving early in the morning, despite Alex's trying to talk her into staying.

He needed to fix things, but it seemed as if the more he tried, the worse things got. On their way to the private plane he'd realized the only thing that would help was to allow her to have a little distance. So he'd obeyed her wishes and let her return to Liam without him.

The funny thing was, he would've thought that after making such a mess of things that he would've been wracked with regret for having ventured into territory into which he'd sworn he'd never enter. But he wasn't sorry that he'd proposed. His only regret was that he wished he'd had the clarity last night that he possessed this morning.

Truth be told, last night he hadn't been one-hundred-percent positive that marriage was the right thing. But watching Julianne walk out of his bedroom without even a backward glance at him, he'd known that he wanted her more than was rationally possible in a man.

He missed her and his son.

He missed *them*—the two of them; and *them* as a family. He had to figure out a way to convince her that she wanted *them,* too.

Alex finally let his mind and his heart work together to come up with a plan to do just that.

What had she done?

When Alex had first brought up going to Paris with him, she'd had the right response: no. But she'd been an idiot not only going back to Paris, but also sleeping with him.

She'd deluded herself into believing that she knew him, but how could she know him if she'd missed the small fact that he didn't believe in love?

He was Liam's father. He would be in Liam's

life and therefore he would be part of her life, too. There was no getting around it. If she knew what was best for all of them, she'd keep things friendly and platonic.

Period.

The problem, she decided, as she paced around her palace suite, was she felt like a caged animal. Even though she'd kept up with her daily practicing—except for a lapse during the time she spent in Paris with Alex—she needed to be doing something to get her career back on track.

She'd spent too much time at Maya's shop. While friendship was a good thing right now, it was time to focus and get her career back on track. She sat down with a legal pad to prioritize a to-do list.

She'd already met with the director of the St. Michel National Symphony as Henri had arranged, but Maestro Fernand Leroy wasn't auditioning flutes at the moment.

Henri was in the middle of bringing in a huge exhibit of Renaissance painters. He assured her that as soon as the exhibit was up and going that they'd meet with Sophie to talk about the fundraiser for A World of Music.

She called Graham and learned that there was no news to report—the reorganization was still in a holding pattern, waiting for confirmation of grants and donors.

"Isn't there anything I can do on this end to help?" she asked.

"Keep your eyes and ears open for sponsors. Other than that, try to get paying gigs with smaller ensembles to keep yourself afloat in the meantime."

Easy for him to say.

She could make some calls on this end, but the likelihood of her finding European patrons for an American orchestra were slim to none.

Her hands were tied.

She felt as if she'd been rendered utterly useless in her St. Michel ivory tower.

More than a week had gone by since the Paris debacle, and Alex still wasn't home. He'd called to check on Liam, but her own emotions had clouded her perspective, keeping her from being able to even guess at how he felt. They'd simply been ludicrously, frigidly civil to each other, talking about nothing other than Liam.

Had he really asked her to marry him?

It seemed like a distant bad dream.

The most curious part was that she found herself missing him at the oddest times: like when she passed the sailboats at the yacht club; when she looked at the beat-up Bundy case that was still sitting on the entryway table, stuck in the same holding pattern that she was in.

There was no need to mail it home because there was no one in her one-woman office to receive it; and because of that, it would make more sense to carry it home rather than mail it.

Most strongly, she longed for Alex's conversation and companionship at night when she found herself sitting on the couch in front of the fire holding Liam. In silence.

So much time alone gave her too much time to think—time that until now had been scarce.

When she wasn't thinking of Alex, the riddle that had taken over her memory of Marissa occupied Julianne's mind.

What was the real story behind the story told by the sister Julianne had loved and admired?

Now that she knew Alex as well as she did, the one conclusion she kept coming back to was that Marissa hadn't told Alex about the baby because she hadn't wanted to change her life—not even for the good of her own son. Marissa had stuck her newborn baby with a nanny in a war-torn country while she did her fieldwork in a dangerous place. Alex would never have agreed to let his baby stay with a paid babysitter in a war zone. While

Julianne couldn't let herself believe that Marissa was a neglectful mother, the fact remained that Liam hadn't had any of the basic vaccinations and medical screenings most three-month-old American children received. Maybe her sister hadn't gotten around to it. Julianne had to believe that because she still loved Marissa, loved her sister's sense of daring and adventurous personality, but she had to accept the fact that deep down, the sister she loved so much had been selfish. She put herself first, not caring how her decisions affected Alex, Julianne or even Liam.

Sometimes the truth was a bitter pill to swallow.

A small clearing of the clouds happened two days later when Julianne got a call from the artistic director for the Wallansky Orchestra, a regional orchestra for which she'd auditioned before the Continental Symphony Orchestra's European tour. Since the situation with the Continental Symphony Orchestra had seemed shaky, many of the musicians were auditioning, trying to secure stable positions.

Initially, she hadn't won the spot with the Wallansky, but apparently the flutist they'd chosen had been hired away by another orchestra—the subtext being there was *a larger, better paying, more stable orchestra.*

The spot was open again, and they were inviting the musicians who'd ranked in the top four under the initial winner to come back to reaudition. That would happen in two weeks; the decision would be handed down immediately after that.

It certainly wasn't a spot with the New York Philharmonic, but it was something. If she got the job, she and Alex would be forced to make a decision about where Liam would live.

Of course, who knew if the Wallansky came with a an angel like Anita Collins. Julianne might have been naive when it came to Alex Lejardin, but she wouldn't give herself false hope when it came to a new position with a new orchestra. The chance of the added bonus of free child care was slim.

Musical families like she had with the Continental Symphony were few and far between. She'd have to seriously weigh the pros and cons before she auditioned for the new position.

She thanked the artistic director over the phone and promised to let him know within forty-eight hours whether she'd audition.

Alex didn't want to give Julianne any warning that he was coming home, mainly because he hadn't wanted to scare her away. Not that he thought she'd leave St. Michel—but he was being extra cautious in the wake of last week's disaster.

This time, unlike during the trip to Paris, he had a plan. He was going to win her heart.

He knocked on the gilded door of her suite.

When she answered and saw him standing there he could have sworn her initial reaction was a flash of you're-back happiness that was too quickly veiled by cool reserve.

"May I come in for just a moment?" he asked.

"Of course."

"I'm not going to stay, but I wanted to say hello, and see Liam, and tell you that I missed you."

She looked down after he said the last three words, and her long lashes hid the expression in her eyes.

"Liam is sleeping right now, but feel free to go in and take a peek at him if you'd like."

He hesitated a moment in the foyer. "The other reason I'm here is to ask you if you'd please have dinner with me tonight. I've missed you. Savannah will watch the baby."

Her eyes clouded. "Alex, I don't think that's a good idea given what happened last time."

"We'll be fine. I'll be a perfect gentleman. I have some things I need to tell you."

When she hesitated, looking as if she might decline, he added, "It's important."

That night, a limo took Alex and Julianne to the yacht club. The ride was a little strained because she was nervous about seeing him and about hearing the things he wanted to tell her. It sounded so serious. But during the ride Alex poured champagne and made conversation about his work in Paris, and asked questions about Liam and what they'd done since he'd seen them last.

"I have a callback audition for the Wallansky Orchestra, a regional orchestra based in Connecticut."

Alex seemed taken aback for a moment, but then he finally raised his champagne glass in toast to her. "Congratulations."

As she clinked glasses with him, he smiled, but somehow the sentiment didn't quite reach his eyes.

She waited for him to go on the defensive to tell her she couldn't take Liam, but he didn't. That left her feeling anxious and off kilter.

"When is the audition?" he asked instead.

"In two weeks, but I haven't committed to going...yet."

His face brightened a little, but then he returned his gaze to his glass.

"Well, anything we can do to help you..."

As they entered the restaurant and followed the maître d' to a table overlooking the water, Julianne pondered Alex's offer to help. She didn't really know what she wanted him to say instead of that, but it felt as if he were offering to help to pack her bags or—

"In Paris you said you wanted to know the real me," he said suddenly breaking the silence. "The real me isn't happy that you might go. Okay? That's the real me. I'm sorry, I want to be happy for you, but the real me thinks the possibility of your being an ocean away is unbearable."

He paused as if he were waiting for her to react, but she just sat there watching him.

"The real me wants you to know that I understand how you could have doubts about my relationship with Marissa. That's understandable since we made Liam. But I don't know how to convince you that Marissa and I really were *just friends*.

"I guess I could dig up old friends of hers to corroborate my story—to tell you that over the two years I knew your sister, we were not romantically involved, except for that one night.

"One night."

There was such earnestness on his face. Julianne didn't know what to say—and she didn't want to say much, because she didn't want to stop Alex from saying more.

"Having Liam, I can't say that I wish it had never happened," he said.

"Because you love him."

Alex closed his eyes and drew in a ragged breath, looking like a man who was trying to steady himself. "The real me wishes he could tell you that I love you, but honestly I don't know if I'm capable of that emotion. I don't want to lie to you, Julianne. When my mom died, something inside me shut down. Or maybe it died with her, I don't know. Maybe it's a genetic defect or because through my job I've seen too much ugliness.

"All I know is that you and Liam are the best things that have ever happened to me. My life would be so much less without you. Where love factors into that, I don't know. Does it really need a label?"

Julianne kept her eyes on Alex, although his image wavered through the unshed tears that filled her eyes.

"No, Alex, not a label, but what I need is some assurance that I'm not going to fall in love with you and then lose you down the road one day when you

meet the woman who finally wakes up your heart.
Because when that happens mine will break."

"You said that to him?" Maya asked as she
poured a second round of chocolate from a small
brass pot.

Julianne nodded.

"And how did he respond?" She picked up her
cup and sipped, keeping eager eye contact over the
rim of the cobalt-and-white demitasse.

"He said both of us knew that nothing was
guaranteed."

Maya scrunched up her pert nose. "What? What
kind of an answer is that?"

"I know. I believe that he cares, but where does
that leave us? He didn't bring up the proposal
again. And even if he did, I don't know if I could
accept. To me, the definition of hell is to be in a
one-sided marriage."

Maya shook her head in disagreement. "I
don't know, though. I feel you two. You belong
together."

Even though Maya claimed to have a sixth sense
when it came to matchmaking, Julianne had a
sneaking suspicion that a good majority of what
Maya *saw* and *felt* were situations she only wished
would work out.

It was amazing what the power of persuasion could do.

The door chimed and a group of five walked in.

"Ooh, customers," Julianne said. "Let me know if I can help."

Much to Julianne's surprise, they were Americans. Maya greeted them and immediately started handing out samples and answering questions.

How exciting. It was the first time Julianne had seen *anyone* set foot inside Maya's shop other than Alex, Liam and herself, and Alex had been there only that first day.

Liam was sound asleep in his stroller, oblivious to the hubbub in the store.

Then another family of four entered the shop, and then six more people. With fifteen customers, plus Maya and Liam in his stroller, Julianne found the space to be a bit tight. Even so, since Liam was settled, Julianne covered him with his blanket, made eye contact with the bodyguard who waited outside watching through the window, and jumped into the fray to help.

According to the customers, a tour bus had dropped them off to spend the morning. Maya said she'd never gotten a bus this early in the season. Julianne got quite a different perspective of the chocolate business going from zero to fifteen customers, but she still thought it was fun.

Julianne glanced over at Liam, who had turned over on his side, still asleep and snugly covered up.

While Julianne poured hot chocolate into proper demitasse cups for the customers at the iron tables, and filled chocolate orders, she had a fleeting thought that maybe she should wheel Liam's stroller around behind the counter, but it was so busy and the store was so crowded that she decided he'd be fine where he was. She could see him from this angle and the bodyguard had another vantage point.

Then a man asked Julianne to make him a basket to take back to his girlfriend. "But I'm in kind of a rush," he said. "We have to be back on the bus in fifteen minutes."

The guy proceeded to ask about nearly every chocolate in the shop, beckoning Julianne here and there before finally scrapping the basket altogether and opting for a box of dark chocolate truffles decorated with candied violets.

As she rang up his purchase, she was both exhausted and exhilarated. She told Maya that perhaps rather than going back to the States to audition for the Wallansky Orchestra, she could help out in the shop until an opportunity opened with the St. Michel National.

As Maya stood next to her waiting her turn at the register, Julianne said, "There's always the possibility of forming a chamber group, seeing how I still owe you an in-shop live music performance—"

A loud commotion erupted near the door.

Four Secret Service agents lunged over the tables, knocking over iron chairs in the process of getting to Liam's stroller.

The guy who was purchasing the sugared violets threw them at Julianne and dashed for the door.

Chapter Thirteen

Julianne opened her groggy eyes and blinked as she tried to see through the dark gloom of her bedroom. It all seemed like a terrible dream, but then reality set in and the tears started rolling down her cheeks. Again.

How could she ever forgive herself? What kind of a mother—or even an aunt—or any kind of caregiver of a little boy—takes her eyes off a sleeping baby in public, even for a second?

"Julianne?" Alex's voice sounded, soft and soothing from the dark corner of her room. She squinted and saw his silhouette as he stood up and walked toward her.

She turned her face into the pillow and sobbed.

It didn't matter that Secret Service had been watching—well, actually, it did matter. Thank God for the St. Michel Secret Service because Liam was safe, if a little frightened at first.

It had all happened so fast—the sugared violets man had been working in tandem with a rather nondescript guy who'd been sitting at the table closest to Liam's stroller. Neither Maya nor Julianne could remember who'd served the guy at the table the chocolate, but while Sugared Violets distracted Julianne, Hot Chocolate tried to covertly snatch Liam from his stroller, replacing him with a medium-sized teddy bear.

And while Julianne had been too distracted, giddily planning her future as a flute-playing shopgirl, two Vonisian operatives from the terrorist group that had been issuing death threats against Alex, tried to kidnap Liam.

Julianne felt Alex's hand on her back. She wanted to pull away because she didn't deserve comfort. But she couldn't move—and she wasn't sure if it was because she was nearly paralyzed by guilt or still reacting to the sedatives.

So Alex rubbed her back and she sobbed.

She'd been so high and mighty thinking Alex's

insistence on having Secret Service/bodyguards was excessive. Of course, after she'd heard about what happened to his poor mother, she thought Alex was simply shell-shocked from the trauma of losing his mother so violently when he was so young.

Julianne hadn't reacted so extremely to the loss of all the other family members she'd loved. All of them gone. Dead. Buried. Well, not every single one. Not Liam. Thank God, not Liam.

It had been a long night, but Alex believed the worst was over. The terrorists were in custody and would be prosecuted to the fullest extent of the law.

Julianne had been so distraught, he hadn't wanted to leave her alone with Liam. Sophie, as gentle and kind as always, had assigned a nurse to watch over Liam, who was safe and sound asleep in his crib, while Alex sat with Julianne.

The nurse had given her a sedative to calm her down and she'd been in and out of sleep, dozing only fitfully and crying when she was awake.

Alex felt curiously calm.

Liam and Julianne were safe.

They'd made it. They hadn't been harmed—at least not physically.

This strange calm that was enveloping Alex was almost like an endorphin high that didn't make sense. He certainly wasn't reveling in the fact that the two people he loved most in this world had suffered such a trauma.

The two people he loved. Yes. That was it.

He was calm and content because something in him had shifted. It was like a valve in his heart had suddenly been opened and what he was feeling was so strong and good that he didn't ever want to stop feeling it.

It was a damn shame that it took a near-loss to make him come to his senses. He'd been given a second chance at this and this time he wasn't going to blow it.

He kissed his sleeping beauty's forehead and said, "I love you, Julianne."

Her answer was the steady, rhythmic sound of sleep.

A week later, at the New Hampton, Connecticut, Performing Arts Center Julianne sat in the Green Room with the three other musicians who were her competition for the principal flute position with the Wallansky Orchestra. They'd finished the audition and had been waiting for the results for forty-five minutes.

What was taking them so long?

But really, what were a few more minutes' wait after all she gone through to get here?

It had taken her a few days to get a hold of herself, but she'd come around. Despite how Alex and Luc had reinforced that there was nothing she could've done to prevent the kidnapping short of not leaving the palace—and that wasn't practical—Julianne continued to blame herself.

If she'd only wheeled Liam back behind the counter like her gut had been telling her.

"Then who knows how it would've gone down?" Alex said. "The perpetrators were armed. As it happened, they did not feel threatened and did not draw their weapons. If you'd moved Liam, they might have drawn their weapons and ordered everyone to the ground." He abruptly stopped. "Who knows what might have happened. Luckily, we'll never know."

But Julianne knew what real fear was. She'd continued to blame herself; and she didn't trust.

"What if it happens again?"

"Are you afraid?" Alex had asked her.

"Not for myself, but for Liam, I am. Maybe he's better off without me. Everyone I've ever loved has died tragically."

That's when she decided to take the audition. She'd let fate decide where she should be.

If she was good for Liam, she'd lose the audition again and go back to St. Michel.

If she won the audition…well, that meant Liam was better off with his father and family with only occasional visits from her.

She loved him and the thought of not holding him and hugging him and telling him she loved him on a daily basis tore her apart. But this was not about what was good for her. It was about Liam.

And Alex.

She loved Alex, but he couldn't return her feelings and didn't need her complicating his life.

That is, unless fate decided differently.

A dour-looking woman appeared in the doorway of the Green Room and all four musicians sat up straight.

She informed them that she would be calling their names in no significant order. They would each be assigned to a different room where they would report and simultaneously receive the news on whether they made it or not.

The woman called the other three names first and assigned them rooms.

"Julianne Waterford?"

"Yes?" She raised her hand in an anxious greeting even though she was the only one left.

"You may proceed to room number four."

Maybe it was a long trip, but Alex had been determined to bring Liam to New Hampton, to be there for Julianne's audition. Either way the audition went, she'd want her family there to support her—to cheer with her if she won the audition; or to cheer her up if she didn't.

She'd still been shaken about the attempted kidnapping and had been talking nonsense about letting fate decide whether she stayed in St. Michel or left him and Liam to move to New Hampton.

The doctor she'd seen had suggested to Alex that she might be suffering from post-traumatic stress disorder, but Julianne had said she felt fine. Because she didn't seem as if she'd be a harm to herself, the doctor gave her medical clearance to travel for the audition.

She had no idea that Alex and Liam—and a troop of Secret Service agents—had followed right behind her. What other choice did they have? When she'd physically turned and walked away from Liam to get on their plane, she and the boy had both cried. It was a traumatic scene that Alex never wanted to see repeated.

He held his son and watched her go, unable to bring himself to share his newfound feelings until the right moment.

Telling someone he loved her was no small feat for Alex Lejardin. This time, he wanted to make sure he got this one right.

He'd known then that the right time had come, so here he stood, Liam on his hip, a bouquet of red roses in one hand and his son's diaper bag dangling from his shoulder. He drew in a deep breath as he waited, waited to hear his and Liam's fate, which would be decided by Julianne's audition.

An orchestra member had been gracious enough to let them in and point out the elevator from which the candidates would probably be leaving.

A woman with a flute case exited the elevator, but she wasn't Julianne. He couldn't read her expression to know whether she was the one they chose. She looked pretty young for the part, but what did he know?

Liam was gurgling to himself and cooing, "Dadadadada." Alex bounced him and patted a soft, nervous cadence on his little back.

"Mama," Liam said, pointing behind Alex.

Alex whirled around and saw a wide-eyed Julianne staring back at him.

"What—?" she stammered and ran up to them

wrapping them in a bear hug that made Liam giggle. "Oh, my dear God, what on earth are you doing here?"

Alex smiled. "Liam couldn't stand being an ocean away from his mother. And Liam's father won't let an ocean come between him and the woman he loves—and will always love, with his whole heart."

Her hand fluttered to her mouth, then she leaned in and kissed Alex before she took Liam, hugged him and swung him around.

When she'd finally settled down, Alex exchanged the flowers for Liam.

"These are beautiful," she said, sniffing the bouquet. "Thank you."

Finally, Alex couldn't stand the suspense any longer.

"Julianne, what's the verdict? Did you get the position?"

They locked gazes for a moment before a slow smile spread over her face. "Yes, I did."

Alex's insides felt as if they'd been flash frozen. But he sucked up his distress and said, "I'm happy for you. Congratulations." He stared at her beautiful face, hoping disappointment didn't show in his eyes.

"I could try to work out something with

iWITNESS. Perhaps we could open an office in New York. I could commute from Connecticut. That is if you want Liam and me here…with you." He shrugged. "When do you start?"

She laughed.

"It certainly would be easier for both of us to move our headquarters to St. Michel, don't you think? I'm a one-woman office. You have staff and all those files."

Alex squinted at her. "What do you mean?"

She shook her head. "They may have offered me the position in the orchestra, but I didn't say I accepted it."

It took a moment for her words to sink in. When they did, Alex let out a whoop that startled Liam, but when Alex grabbed them into a hug and swung both of them around, Liam let loose a belly laugh that made them all laugh.

"So, why not?" he asked, almost afraid to hear the answer, though he couldn't imagine what could be any worse than her living on the other side of the Atlantic.

"Are you kidding? As much as I'd love to play with the Wallansky Orchestra, there will be other orchestras. Maybe even—hopefully in time— something with the St. Michel National Orchestra. What's most important is that right now Liam needs to be in St. Michel with his entire family. Sophie, Luc, Henri, you and me. And I can't leave my two guys—not even for the time it would take to move the iWITNESS headquarters here."

Her words were enough to melt him from the inside out. He dipped his head and kissed her soundly on the mouth and she kissed him back.

"I love you," he said.

She beamed up at him. "I love you, too. Are you ready to go home?"

"Not quite," Alex said. "Before we go back to St. Michel, we have a stop to make."

She frowned her confusion. "Where do we need to go?"

Balancing Liam on his hip, he reached into the diaper bag and pulled out the battered Bundy flute case.

"I've been carting this flute around since I left Paris. I'd like to find someone who could put it to good use. Preferably a child in Washington, D.C. Since that's where A World of Music was founded."

Julianne looked genuinely touched as she took the instrument from him. "Thank you. I thought about bringing it, but then I decided I'd wait and see what happened with the audition. Especially since Washington is more than three hundred miles away. I wasn't exactly going to be in the neighborhood this time. I figured I'd deliver it when I went home to pack up my apartment."

Alex quirked a brow.

"Well, there's no time like the present. And my plane just happens to be stopping in D.C. I'll help you pack. And this time I will be exchanging a flute for the opportunity to share a life with a person I love."

As they kissed again, Liam cooed, "Love. Love. Love. Love. Mama. Dada."

* * * * *

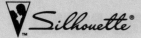

COMING NEXT MONTH

Available July 27, 2010

SPECIAL EDITION

REQUEST YOUR FREE BOOKS!
2 FREE NOVELS PLUS 2 FREE GIFTS!

SPECIAL EDITION
Life, Love and Family!

HARLEQUIN®

A Romance

FOR EVERY MOOD™

Spotlight on
Heart & Home

Heartwarming romances
where love can happen
right when you least expect it.

See the next page to enjoy a sneak peek
from Harlequin® American Romance®,
a Heart and Home series.

*Five hunky Texas single fathers—five stories from
Cathy Gillen Thacker's* LONE STAR DADS *miniseries.
Here's an excerpt from the latest,* THE MOMMY PROPOSAL
from Harlequin American Romance.

"I hear you work miracles," Nate Hutchinson drawled. Brooke Mitchell had just stepped into his lavishly appointed office in downtown Fort Worth, Texas.

"Sometimes, I do." Brooke smiled and took the sexy financier's hand in hers, shook it briefly.

"Good." Nate looked her straight in the eye. "Because I'm in need of a home makeover—fast. The son of an old friend is coming to live with me."

She was still tingling from the feel of his warm palm. "Temporarily or permanently?"

"If all goes according to plan, I'll adopt Landry by summer's end."

Brooke had heard the founder of Nate Hutchinson Financial Services was eligible, wealthy and generous to a fault. She hadn't known he was in the market for a family, but she supposed she shouldn't be surprised. But Brooke had figured a man as successful and handsome as Nate would want one the old-fashioned way. *Not that this was any of her business…*

"So what's the child like?" she asked crisply, trying not to think how the marine-blue of Nate's dress shirt deepened the hue of his eyes.

"I don't know." Nate took a seat behind his massive antique mahogany desk. He relaxed against the smooth leather of the chair. "I've never met him."

"Yet you've invited this kid to live with you permanently?"

"It's complicated. But I'm sure it's going to be fine."

Obviously Nate Hutchinson knew as little about teenage

boys as he did about decorating. But that wasn't her problem. Finding a way to do the assignment without getting the least bit emotionally involved was.

Find out how a young boy brings Nate and Brooke
together in THE MOMMY PROPOSAL,
coming August 2010 from Harlequin American Romance.

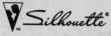

ROMANTIC

S U S P E N S E

Sparked by Danger, Fueled by Passion.

SILHOUETTE ROMANTIC SUSPENSE BRINGS YOU
AN ALL-NEW COLTONS OF MONTANA STORY!

FBI agent Jake Pierson is determined to solve his case,
even if it means courting and using the daughter of a
murdered informant. Mary Walsh hates liars and,
now that Jake has fallen deeply in love, he is afraid
to tell her the truth. But the truth is not the only
thing out there to hurt Mary…

Be part of the romance and suspense in

Covert Agent's Virgin Affair

by

LINDA CONRAD

Available August 2010 where books are sold.

Visit Silhouette Books at www.eHarlequin.com

SRS27690

HARLEQUIN *Presents*

The *Balfour* *Brides*

A powerful dynasty,
eight daughters in disgrace…

Absolute scandal has rocked the core of the infamous
Balfour family. The glittering, gorgeous daughters are in
disgrace…. Banished from the Balfour mansion, they're
sent to the boldest, most magnificent men
to be wedded, bedded…and tamed!

And so begins a scandalous saga of dazzling glamour
and passionate surrender.